# Hiding

## by

## Katherine McDermott

This is a work of fiction. Names, characters, places, and incidents are either the product of the author's imagination or are used fictitiously, and any resemblance to actual persons living or dead, business establishments, events, or locales, is entirely coincidental.

**Hiding**

Cover Art by *Kim Mendoza*

The Wild Rose Press, Inc.
PO Box 708
Adams Basin, NY 14410-0708
Visit us at www.thewildrosepress.com

Publishing History
First Crimson Rose Edition, 2015
Print ISBN 978-1-5092-0285-0
Digital ISBN 978-1-5092-0286-7

Published in the United States of America

**Alex illuminated the crypt**
with his light, and Teresa tried to interpret what she
saw: uneven walls, a doorway surrounded by orbs, a
floor littered with dried reeds. No, they weren't reeds;
they were bones. And the orbs were skulls! The
catacombs! Her heart pounded in her chest like a
jackhammer. Alex had withdrawn his knife. The blade
glittered in the dim light of the torch which cast
luminous shadows on the walls. *What better place to
kill someone? What was another set of bones among the
many? Lord, as you helped the Christians long ago who
met secretly in catacombs, help me.*

## Praise for Katherine McDermott

Ms. McDermott received the RWA Kiss of Death Chapter Daphne du Maurier Award of Excellence in 2012 for an unpublished Romantic Mystery/Suspense.

She also received Honorable Mention Inspirational Romance for another one of her manuscripts in the 2013 Great Expectations Contest by the North Texas chapter of Romance Writers of America.

# Dedication

To my husband,
who has put up with hours of typing,
and to my friends.

Chapter One

"Do you see how this shadow falls beneath her chin?" Teresa showed John the shaded area on the model's neck.

"Yes," he answered, blending a touch of burnt sienna into the fleshy mixture of paint already on his palette before applying it to his canvas.

"You're doing an excellent job," Teresa said. Standing behind him, she critically assessed his progress. Beyond the canvas, she recognized Alex waiting in the doorway with dark, glowering eyes and a clenched jaw. She glanced at her wristwatch.

"I guess our time is up," she said. "You have real talent."

"You inspire me in ways I never thought possible," John said. "I actually see that I'm making progress. I'm sorry the course is ending." He put his arm around her shoulders and gave her a friendly squeeze.

Her other students, Tim, Janine, Marian, and a sixty-five-year-old retiree, Stella, took their brushes to the stainless steel sink to wash out the paint. Teresa watched the colors swirl together as they washed down the drain. The airy room on the second floor of the community arts center smelled of paint and turpentine from the oils class across the corridor.

"Nicole, thank you," Teresa said to the auburn-haired model who had sat perfectly still in the glare of a

1

spotlight while they sketched and painted.

"Sure. Call me again sometime when you need me." She flipped a strand of long hair over her shoulder.

Teresa packed her own tubes of acrylic paint and sable brushes into her tote. Classes throughout the community center were leaving. The halls filled with students exiting dance classes, guitar jam sessions, and sculpting studios.

"That guy is hitting on you," Alex said as they rode the elevator to the bottom floor.

"No, he wasn't, Alex." She hated his unfounded jealousy.

"I saw the way he looked at you. The next thing you know, he'll ask you to model for him privately."

"I wouldn't do that," she replied.

The elevator jarred to a halt, and the metal doors drew apart. Alex seized her upper arm gruffly and propelled her toward the silver Honda Accord in the dim parking lot. All the way to her apartment, he drove in sullen silence, his black brows drawn together in a hostile line.

Sitting next to him, Teresa's stomach clenched. When they reached the Oaks Plantation Apartments complex, traditional brick colonials with white columns and balconies, Teresa bolted from the car. His door slammed behind her.

He grabbed her shoulders roughly and turned her to him. His insolent, vengeful kiss claimed her as his rightful property.

Teresa pulled back. "I'm really tired," she said, her hand placed gently on his chest, a simple gesture of restraint. "I'm going to bed early."

"You're meeting him somewhere, aren't you?" Alex's dark eyes flashed. Normally handsome in a rugged sort of way, his eyes crackled with rage.

"No, I'm not." She sighed as she walked upstairs her apartment, key in hand. Alex's footsteps sounded behind her. At the last moment, she looked back, and he struck her across the cheek with a loud smack, wrenching her neck. Her tote fell, scattering art supplies over the carpeted corridor. She tasted blood at the corner of her mouth.

Trembling, she forced her voice to remain steady. "Go home, Alex," she warned.

He jerked her to him.

"Stop it!" She heard the edge of panic in her voice.

There might have been a bigger row if her neighbor, a former army captain, had not come out of his apartment.

"Is there a problem, Miss Worthington?" Captain Jeffers asked. His well-defined chin jutted forward, and his blue eyes narrowed. A crew cut and a tight fitting T-shirt that sculpted strong abs and powerful chest muscles bespoke a trained soldier.

"No," Teresa said, embarrassed by the scene. "Not anymore. Thank you."

Alex hesitated as if he might punch the captain, then thought better of it, turned, and bounded down the stairs as she gathered her paints and brushes. It wasn't the first time that he'd hit her. But it would be the last.

After her father's death from cancer in Chapin, South Carolina, Teresa had considered Alex Sinclair a godsend at first. A financial advisor by profession, he had helped make sense of her financial situation, aided her through probate, and even lent her money. But then

3

he had slowly tightened his grip taking for granted they were a couple when she still reeled from grief and confusion.

She had moved from Columbia to Charleston, South Carolina, hoping to distance herself and regain her independence. But he'd followed her, insisting that she needed his help with transportation since she had no car. He undermined her confidence. She supposed he considered her ungrateful. But she would not stand for any more abuse. This time she would go farther, some place he wouldn't find her.

Inside she locked and bolted the door. Then with a sigh, she rested her back against the hard wood and closed her eyes for a brief moment. Finally, she went into the bathroom to examine her face in the mirror above the sink.

She touched the swollen, red mark beneath her eye.

"Never again," she said aloud to her reflection. "Never again," she repeated with more strength, more conviction. She balled her fists with resolve. Hot tears rolled down her cheeks as she took a tissue and dabbed blood from her lip. "Never, never again."

This time she'd go to the city known for its ability to understand the soul of an artist—Paris. With a one-way ticket to France, she would break all contact with Alex Sinclair. Her father's loss of work, hospital expenses, and funeral had left only a small amount in savings. But it would purchase a fare to France. She was glad now that she had applied for a visa a month ago hoping to pursue employment in Paris.

She retrieved a battered but sturdy suitcase from the back of the closet, tossed it on the bed, and packed. Her passport was current because she had always wanted to see France with its art museums, Monet's home and pond of water lilies, the Seine.

Her job prospects were as good in Paris as in Charleston, and she'd tell no one where she was going. She looked up the phone number for Delta Airlines, made the call, and purchased a one-way ticket. She'd have only two thousand dollars when she emptied her bank account in the morning, but there would be an ocean between herself and her stalker.

Too excited to sleep, she tossed and turned alternating between fetal and pretzel positions. Fear crept in like a black cat in the shadows. Where would she live? She didn't know a soul in Paris, and her French was elementary at best. What if Alex found her? Amid these worries, she dozed fitfully.

When morning arrived, she printed two dozen résumés from her laptop. The outmoded printer would have to stay behind, but the laptop went in the suitcase. Next she scribbled a note to the landlord citing a family emergency from which she would not be returning and left it on the table with her key. She called a cab to take her to the Charleston International Airport. Then, wheeling her suitcase with one arm and toting her art case in the other, she walked to the parking lot, her gaze darting about in case Alex lurked in the shadows.

"Please take me to the ATM at Bank of America on Sam Rittenberg," she told the cab driver when he arrived. "After that, the airport."

After paying the driver and checking her bag, she went through airport security, placing her pocketbook on a conveyor belt for x-ray, removing her shoes, and allowing a TSA employee to scan her with a wand. As she waited in the terminal, the magnitude of her decision overwhelmed her. She had to gather all her determination and courage to enter the plane when her flight number was called.

On the long flight, she read magazines and worked crossword puzzles to keep her mind occupied. Finally, she napped.

Nine hours later, she arrived at Charles de Gaulle Airport. Guards of the national gendarmerie with automatic weapons carefully watched the terminal. Since 9/11 security around the world stayed alert. At the Bureau de Change, she converted one thousand dollars to euros. *I must be frugal.* The small, inexpensive hotel she'd selected through the Internet on her mobile stood on Boulevard Garibaldi. Fortunately, January was considered the off season.

"*Parlez-vous l'anglais?*" she ventured timidly at the window.

"*Oui,*" the man with a prominent nose and thinning hair replied.

"Can you advise me which train to take?"

"To where are you traveling?" he asked with a nasal accent.

"Garibaldi Boulevard."

Referring to the electronic Paris Métro public transit system map on the wall, he traced the route.

"It is not too difficult," he assured her.

She maneuvered her unwieldy suitcase like an elephant as she embarked on the train. Once on board, she sat in a dim corner and watched the passing scenery of terminals with French advertisements posted on walls. In spite of the heavy foundation she'd applied, she wondered if anyone noticed her bruised cheek.

The train stopped briefly, and other passengers

boarded. A tall Frenchman ripe with the potent odor of perspiration sat next to her. His eyes traversed her figure with lecherous interest.

An irrational fear made her tense.

"*Pardonnez-moi.*" She made a hasty exit toward the restroom before choosing another seat next to a harmless, elderly woman.

As the transport neared the teeming heart of Paris, it rose up an elevated track. At her station, Teresa disembarked and dragged her luggage down the stairs. Under the stairwell, two drunks slept off an all-nighter using their rolled up jackets as makeshift pillows. *Probably homeless, but not dangerous. Every large city has its vagrants.* The stale smell of alcohol and urine permeated the air.

Directly across the street stood the outmoded, brick hotel, but the surrounding area looked clean. The wide avenue lined with shady poplars produced a soothing effect. Though a chilly wind swept the boulevard, cyclists and pedestrians strolled about amiably.

She pushed open the door beneath the French tricolor flag. Inside, the concierge looked up and smiled. Wavy, ash brown hair fell over a smooth forehead that dropped off to a long, narrow nose. His tanned skin implied a love for the outdoors.

"*Bonjour.* Welcome to the Garibaldi." A warm smile lit his lively Mediterranean blue eyes and made deep dimples in both cheeks. "*Je m'appelle* Serge Gervais. How can I be of service to you?"

"I should have a reservation, Monsieur Gervais," Teresa said.

When he saw that she spoke English, he immediately switched to her language with fluent ease.

"Just let me check the computer. Your name?"

"Teresa Worthington."

"Yes, I see here a room with a single bed. Your credit card?"

"No!" Teresa cried out the word. She mustn't give Alex any way to trace her. "I mean, I'd like to pay cash."

"Three nights?"

"Yes, for now," she said.

"That will be a hundred and fifty euros."

Teresa counted out the money, thankful that the exchange from dollars to euros had been in her favor.

Serge handled the payment and then stepped around the corner to take her bags. He had an athletic build with broad shoulders, a strong, lean torso that narrowed to masculine hips. Though he wore a white long sleeved shirt, black pants, and a geometric designed blue tie, Teresa could see beneath the stretched material his thigh muscles were those of a cyclist or swimmer.

"Oh, no," Teresa objected. She couldn't afford to tip him. "If you'll just tell me the room number."

"But you're our guest." He lifted the heavy suitcase as if it were nothing and accompanied her on a narrow elevator that rose to the fifth floor where a small but comfortable room awaited. He looked close to thirty though he had a boyish grin.

"There will be fresh croissants and fruit in the dining room in the morning," he informed her. "*Le petit déjeuner.*"

"*Merci,*" Teresa replied.

"Are you hungry now?"

"I am, a little," Teresa lied. Her stomach growled

bear-like.

"I will bring you *un pain au chocolat*, complimentary." He winked.

He disappeared, and she began to unpack her suitcase. The last person she wanted to become involved with was a charming man. *I must establish my independence.* A rap at the door interrupted her frantic thoughts.

Looking through the tiny peephole, she saw the concierge and unbolted the door. He proffered the chocolate-filled pastry wrapped in a cloth napkin.

"Just remember, it's our secret," he said pressing his forefinger to his lips in an exaggerated gesture of silence.

"Thank you," she said taking the food. "I mean— *merci.*"

"*Bon soir.*" He hesitated momentarily and left.

With the door securely locked, Teresa devoured the scrumptious, chocolate-filled croissant and followed it with a glass of water. On second thought, she wedged a chair beneath the doorknob and pulled the drapes shut. Tomorrow she would find some inexpensive staples, search for a job, and hunt for a cheap apartment, but tonight she would sleep. Looking out the window, she could see a small section of the Eiffel Tower glowing with light—a promise of freedom, a symbol of hope.

\*\*\*\*

Gray dawn peeped through the thin opening between the curtains. Teresa jumped out of bed, took a steaming hot shower, and donned her best outfit, a lavender sweater and print skirt. Then grabbing her scarf and coat, she took the lift to the lobby. She glanced at the front desk to see if Serge was there, but a different employee manned the front desk.

In the small dining room, a buffet awaited: baskets of oranges and bananas, an array of breads and pastries, juices, and crêpes. There were syrupy strawberries and blueberries as well as whipped cream for toppings. Teresa helped herself to two croissants, an orange, and a steaming cup of *café au lait*.

When she finished eating, she ventured across the dining room to the attendant at the desk. Teresa glanced at her name tag.

"Mauricette, I'm looking for work, and I wondered if you knew of anyone seeking help."

"What kind of work?" Mauricette asked in a bored tone.

"Anything really, waitress, secretary. I have a visa. And I have a degree in studio art and a minor in art history from the University of South Carolina."

"Then you might try some of the art museums, the Musée D'Orsay and the Rodin."

"Do you have a map of the city?"

Mauricette pulled a brochure from behind the desk and handed it to Teresa.

"*Merci*," Teresa said.

"*Bonne chance*," Mauricette replied in a sarcastic tone that sounded as though she meant "fat chance."

Abashed and confused by her rudeness, Teresa turned away.

Carrying a folder of resumes, she exited the hotel. Outside, the French national flag flapped in the breeze, its *bleu, blanc, et rouge* bands undulating with the wind. Following the street signs to the Rodin Museum, Teresa walked to a lovely old mansion that reminded her of the von Trapp family home in *The Sound of*

*Music.* Occasionally, she passed bereted Frenchmen with unwrapped baguettes under their arms, the equivalent of grabbing an Egg McMuffin in America.

She picked up an application from the front desk but couldn't help peeking into the rooms filled with statuary: busts of beautiful women, carvings displaying Greek myths, and the *Gates of Hell* in which Rodin's famous sculpture *The Thinker* represented the poet Dante. Beyond an enormous plate glass window, the meticulously maintained garden behind the mansion held more statues and a traditional café. Light snow dusted the grounds. *I'm really in Paris; Alex is far away.* Tension drained from her shoulders.

She sat down, filled in the lengthy application, added her résumé, and returned it to the front desk. Consulting her map, which depicted the concentric avenues of Paris and the numerous *arrondissements*, Teresa realized the walk to Musée d'Orsay would be overwhelming, so she boarded a city bus that rumbled past the military school where Napoleon had trained as a cadet according to the bus driver.

Lines of tourists waited outside the museum to view the Impressionists, Monet, Renoir, and van Gogh. When she told the woman at the ticket office what she wanted, she received another application. Her numb hands made writing difficult.

She left the number of her cell phone, for which she had purchased an international chip, as a contact number.

After she finished at the museum, she strolled up the street introducing herself and leaving a few résumés at sidewalk cafés and fragrant *boulangeries*. Finally, she bought some cans of soup, a copper-bottomed pot., and an electric adapter for her hot plate. Using her bus pass, she returned to the hotel. Mauricette barely looked up from the computer when Teresa entered.

She rode the lift to her floor and used her card key to enter. In no time, the hot plate she had brought from Charleston heated the soup to a boil. The steamy tomato and basil broth warmed her down to her frozen toes.

She pulled back the curtain and looked down on a desolate courtyard with a few rolls of plastic turf strewn haphazardly beneath a single umbrella table.

A tall, concrete fence surrounded the barren lawn. No plants or flowers, no fountains, or statues adorned the enclosure. The artist in her longed to create beauty where none existed. Then, hazarding a guess, she realized the courtyard probably belonged to her hotel. She descended the stairs and found a narrow corridor leading to the courtyard where several hotel workers, including Mauricette, smoked cigarettes in spite of the cold. Back inside, she noticed Serge at the front desk.

"May I help you?" he asked.

"Do you know—I mean is it possible that improvements to the courtyard might be planned?"

"Ugly, isn't it? I keep telling the owner to renovate it before spring and move extra dining tables out there. Why do you ask?"

"I'm an artist, and I'm sure I could paint a very interesting mural for him."

"He'll be back this weekend. Perhaps if you have a portfolio of your work—"

"I do." Teresa pushed a loose strand of honey-colored hair behind her ear.

"Then I'll arrange a meeting, but perhaps you would like to show your paintings to me tonight at dinner. I'm off by eight o'clock."

"No, I don't think so." Her hands shook involuntarily, and Serge noticed.

"No strings, no expectations. I'd really like to see what you do."

"As long as you understand that it's just business," Teresa warned.

"You are very serious, yes?" Serge stifled a laugh.

"Yes, I am," Teresa said with a smidgen of resentment.

"I'll see you at eight o'clock, and I promise you the best Italian food in Paris."

****

Upstairs, Teresa chastised herself. *Why on earth did I say I'd go to dinner with him?* To ease her mounting anxiety, she pulled her sketchbook out of the suitcase and seated herself by the window overlooking the courtyard. Beyond the fence, a tall apartment building rose skyward. Some apartments sported small balconies that also overlooked the courtyard. Several had tables and chairs, small grills, potted plants. On one, a slender woman, about her own age, leaned against the wrought iron railing.

Teresa did not want to spoil the woman's reverie and solitude so she remained hidden behind the sheer curtain. Quickly, she began to sketch a new courtyard with narrow flower beds along the walls, a fountain in one corner and a mural along the back wall depicting a traditional Parisian café with burgundy awning, shady poplars, and tables nestled below protective umbrellas. In the background, a miniature Eiffel Tower glimmered.

Pulling out a box of colored pencils, she drew in

red begonias, purple phlox, and white vincas. Her knowledge of plants came from her father and mother, amateur gardeners who had kept a lovely lawn and garden behind their house. Then, hit by sudden inspiration, Teresa drew in an herb garden where the hotel kitchen could grow its own rosemary, parsley, mint, and oregano. She had places on the wall where hanging baskets of flowers could be mounted.

As she drew, time passed quickly. The heater rattled on and blew the sheers back from the window. The young woman in the opposite building caught a glimpse of her.

Teresa pushed open the window and called out.

"*Bonjour.*"

The woman answered rapidly in fluent French.

"*Pardon,*" Teresa apologized. "*Anglais*?"

"I speak English pretty good," the woman replied. "You are English?"

"No, I'm American. My name is Teresa Worthington."

"Annette Hughes. My husband is British."

"I promise I'm not spying on you," Teresa said. "I'm drawing."

Annette's eyebrows rose. "What were you drawing?"

"An improved courtyard."

Annette laughed. "It is a view unappealing," she agreed. "I'm sorry. My *anglais* is not good. Guy is always correcting me."

"It is wonderful compared to my French," Teresa replied.

"You would like something hot to drink? You would like coffee perhaps? I'm in apartment 410."

"If you're sure it's not an inconvenience."

Putting down her drawing, she donned her wool coat and took the lift down to the lobby, stepped out into the cold and walked around the corner. Annette came down to let her inside the secured entrance. An attractive brunette with the expressive mahogany eyes, Annette led her onto the elevator and into her airy, modern apartment. The inviting aroma of freshly brewed coffee enticed Teresa into the small compartmentalized kitchen.

"I appreciate the invitation," she said. "I don't know anyone here yet."

"I moved here from Lyon," Annette explained. "My husband, Guy, works for L'Oréal. If you need cosmetics, I have, how do you say—examples?"

"I think you mean samples, and I can use all the help I can get." Teresa smiled.

"Your complexion is quite lovely," Annette replied. "Café au lait?'

"Yes, please."

Annette poured milk into the dark liquid steaming in a ceramic mug. Teresa glimpsed an herb garden of potted plants on Annette's window sill. She recognized the small leaves and spicy aroma of oregano.

"I hope to include herbs in the renovation of the courtyard," she said.

"So you've been hired to improve it?"

"Not exactly," Teresa said. "Not yet anyway, but I'm hopeful." She explained the situation, and Annette wished her success.

"If you land the job, I'll help with the herb garden."

"That would be wonderful."

15

"I'm not looking for employment because I'm expecting a baby in May." She patted her swollen abdomen.

"Congratulations!"

"I'm six months along and very nervous. I've had a lot of morning sickness."

"You'll be fine. In the spring, we'll take walks. Exercise will help with labor."

"So will pain medication," Annette said with a laugh.

"One of the perks of modern medicine," Teresa concurred. "Next time you'll come visit me, I hope." She excused herself.

Braving the frigid temperature, she returned to the hotel pink-cheeked and chilled. Serge, assisting another guest, looked up briefly, but Teresa avoided eye contact. She wanted to discourage him from dating, even though he appealed to her. Could she trust her judgment concerning men? For all she knew, he might be married. Supposedly Frenchmen had a tendency to womanize, with a wife at home and a mistress in town.

Upstairs she took a hot shower and let the water massage her muscles. The faint lilac smell of the shampoo provided an aromatic therapy that calmed her nerves. After she'd rinsed her hair, she slid out of the shower and wrapped a towel around her head like a turban. Then she slipped into a maroon blouse and ebony slacks. Fur lined ankle boots would keep her feet warm. Selecting several paintings from her portfolio, she slipped them in a manila folder along with her preliminary sketches of the courtyard. Finally, she turned a blow dryer to her hair and then used a curling iron to force the limp strands to curve under.

A rap drew her to the door. Opening it she noted Serge had donned a tie and a winter coat. His muted aquamarine shirt enhanced the stunningly similar hues in his eyes. *He's definitely handsome,* très beau. *But that just makes him all the more dangerous.* She grabbed her black wool coat.

"You might want a scarf or a hat," he informed her. "Light snow is falling. But don't worry, it's melting when it touches the ground."

Following his advice, Teresa pulled a crimson scarf from her pocket and wound it over her head and around her neck.

"The restaurant is not far. Just two streets over, Felipe's."

Outside, soft flakes gathered on Teresa's shoulders and scarf like confetti. Their breathing appeared in mists of condensation. From the exterior, the restaurant appeared warm and inviting. Inside, the brick red walls and black ceiling fitted with recessed lighting added to the ambience. Italian music played softly over the stereo system evoking European charm.

"The Italian food is fantastic here—lasagna, Alfredo, pizza. They cut the prosciutto they put on the pizza very thin."

Teresa found his enthusiasm contagious. When the waiter had seated them, she perused the menu with interest though she recognized the names of only a few items.

"Egg on pizza?" she questioned.

"Have you ever tried it?"

"No," she admitted.

"When in France—" Serge cocked one eyebrow.

"Do as the Italians do?" she teased.

"*Touché*!" He laughed.

The waiter, a young man with a swarthy complexion and dark coarse hair, took their order.

"We'll split a pizza," Serge said, suddenly inspired. "But only put egg on one half. That way you can try it," he explained to Teresa, "but you're not stuck if you don't like it."

"As you wish." The waiter left to take their order to the kitchen.

"Your English is so good," Teresa observed.

"My mother was American." The candlelight cast flickering shadows over his face. "I'm Franco-American."

Teresa smiled, but as she did, the painful bruise on her cheek nagged her. "Isn't that some sort of canned spaghetti?"

"You have the cutest dimple in your left cheek," he said. The waiter had left a bottle of sparkling water, and Serge poured some into two long-stemmed glasses. "What brings you to Paris?"

"The study and production of art, I hope." Teresa looked away from his mesmerizing blue eyes. "Speaking of which—I brought some samples of my work." She pulled her drawings from the satchel she used as a purse.

Serge studied them. "You are an *artiste naturelle*," he announced. "I especially like this one."

He indicated a watercolor of the Morris Island Lighthouse on the Carolina coast with the sky rosy at sunset. On the ocean drifted various waterfowl. A single boat battled the waves. A V of brown pelicans fanned past the striped tower, and foaming surf splashed against its foundation.

"It's a beach near Charleston, South Carolina, a beautiful, old colonial city with neighboring plantations and a lot of history."

"Do you like to swim at this beach?"

"Yes, I did."

"It reminds me of Nice. My grandparents took me to the beach there in the summer.

"Monsieur la Salle is coming Friday, and it will be my pleasure to show him your work. You need to add an estimate sheet detailing the cost of supplies, your labor, and amount of time you think will be needed to complete the mural. I have to warn you, the man does not like to spend money."

"Yes." She had not thought of the budget and appreciated his advice. Suddenly embarrassed that she might seem inexperienced and naïve, she blushed.

The waiter returned with a delectable pizza already divided into triangular slices. Two fried eggs topped one side. He set it in the center of the table and promised them a gastronomic experience.

Serge lifted two steaming slices onto Teresa's plate, the mozzarella stretching in delicious strings from the original pie.

"For you, mademoiselle," Serge said with gallantry. The aroma of oregano, green peppers, onions, and black olives enticed her.

"*Merci beaucoup*," she replied. The cold weather had whetted her appetite, and she ate enthusiastically, but again experienced a moment of self-consciousness as two long strands of mozzarella cheese swung from her mouth like limp spaghetti noodles. She hurriedly stuffed them inside with her hand.

"You know, I fashion myself an artist of sorts,"

Serge chatted amiably.

"Oh?"

"A culinary artist. I like to cook."

"What a coincidence—I like to eat." Teresa laughed.

"As a chef, I found your idea for an herb garden quite practical. Thyme and oregano for the sauces, rosemary and olive oil for the bread. The job I have now is a steppingstone. When I've saved enough for a down payment, I want to start a restaurant, traditional French cooking that I learned from my grandparents. I'm three-fourths of the way there. It's taken a lot of determination because I'm no spendthrift."

"Then you too have an ambition to pursue."

The waiter returned. "Would you like dessert? I recommend the éclairs." Robust and garrulous, he looked like a man who appreciated good food.

"I couldn't eat another bite," Teresa objected. "It was very good, and I'm more than full. Eggs on pizza are quite delicious."

"Perhaps a dessert coffee?" He turned to Serge.

"*Merci*, no." He waved his hand to ward off any more temptation.

When the bill, *l'addition*, arrived, Teresa insisted on paying her half. "A business meeting," she reminded.

On the way back to the hotel, Serge mused aloud. "I think someone has hurt you, violated your trust. You've built a fence to protect yourself, yes?"

Although impressed with his intuition, Teresa did not want to get personal. "I have a stiff upper lip," she said. "I'll survive."

Serge frowned in bewilderment at the idiom. "Your

lips look pliable enough to me."

"What I need is a friend, just a friend," she said.

"Then a friend you shall have."

In the lobby, she proffered her hand and shook his in a businesslike manner.

"I'll consider you my art agent," she said before entering the elevator.

"I'll serve you to the best of my ability," he replied.

But Teresa feared that his lingering gaze meant he hoped she'd soon consider him much more.

\*\*\*\*

Serge sat back in his chair behind the front desk thinking about Teresa. She amused him, a strange mixture of shyness and spunk, of trepidation and temerity. He remembered the way her eyes lit up when she talked about painting. He recalled the rose and ivory glow of her complexion in the candlelight. He had been tempted to stroke her cheek. No doubt it would have felt as soft as a rose petal. But there was something she didn't want to reveal. Perhaps she had a boyfriend.

*Then why isn't he here?* Questions somersaulted in his mind like acrobats at Cirque du Soleil.

Though he was officially off duty, he crossed to the breakfast area, rearranged the fruit, and tossed a few used sugar packets in the trash. Restless, he checked to make sure sufficient water remained in the vases of flowers on the individual tables.

He sighed, and the familiar pang of dissatisfaction and unhappiness fell over him like a sun-blocking shadow. Then he stood before the window and watched the snow fall. He supposed everyone had their secrets.

*Don't I have my own?*

The old what-if-things-had-been-different question resurfaced. "What-if" was a circuitous road he had traveled over and over down the mountain of hope to the valley of despair. "What-if" was an ephemeral bubble, gently drifting, elusive, and iridescent—then vanishing.

Chapter Two

The long, dimly lit corridor stretched before her. Teresa sensed the presence of a shadowlike, faceless figure around the corner. *I must hide.* But where could she hide against those straight, plain walls? She could hear labored breathing but could see no one. Tentacle-like, something wrapped about her ankle. Screaming, she sat upright in the bed, wet with perspiration and entangled in the sheets. Her chest reverberated with the heavy pounding of her heart.

*I am far away from Alex. He doesn't know where I am. I don't need to be afraid.* Chilled in her damp nightgown, she braved the cold outside the bed with chattering teeth and changed into plaid flannel pajamas. Then huddling beneath the covers, she waited till her body heat warmed the bed.

*Lord, you gave me the courage to come here. Give me the means to survive. I place myself entirely in your care.*

As a distraction, she turned on the television mounted in the upper right corner of the room. She couldn't understand much of the dialogue but thought perhaps it would improve her acquisition of French. Flipping channels with the remote, she was surprised to find many American sitcoms with the actors speaking French. The actors' lines were not synchronized with the movement of the lips, and sometimes there were obvious lags in speech. She laughed at Courtney Fox parlaying with Matt LeBlanc in an episode of *Friends*.

Then she switched stations to an old American Western where the lanky cowboys, the painted Indians, and even the swarthy Mexicans spoke fluent French. Teresa found herself wishing for subtitles. As the black and white images flickered, her eyelids grew heavy, and she drifted back to more restful sleep.

In the morning, she did not feel well. Outside a thick layer of snow covered the courtyard. She took her temperature with a thermometer, 102 degrees. After washing down two aspirins with a glass of tepid water, she climbed back in bed but awoke at noon hungry, thirsty, and aching all over. She called the front desk and felt relieved to hear Serge's familiar voice with its nasal accent.

"*Potage au poulet*," he prescribed and soon came upstairs with a bowl of salty chicken soup.

Teresa had put on a robe and sat in a chair with her bare feet tucked beneath her. The hot broth soothed her sore throat. "I'm sorry to be such trouble," she apologized.

"No trouble," Serge said. "I think you're coming down with a virus."

Suddenly, Teresa's mobile phone sounded. She snapped it open and answered.

"Hello." To her own ears, her voice sounded tentative, even slightly leery. She listened carefully as the secretary on the other end invited her to come in Monday for a job interview at the Rodin Museum at ten a.m.

"I'll be there," she said.

"Good news?" Serge inquired.

"A job interview," she replied.

"Congratulations."

"It's only a part-time position," she said. "But it's something."

"I hope it all goes well." He squeezed her hand. "I have to go back to work, but I'll check on you later."

After he left, Teresa took a steaming shower that opened her sinuses and relieved her aching muscles. Then she climbed back into bed to rest. By six o'clock, her fever had declined, but her head still ached. She switched from aspirin to a decongestant.

Serge brought up an omelet that he had cooked himself and a glass of fresh squeezed orange juice.

"You're so good to me," Teresa said. "No one has ever nursed me when I was sick other than my mother." The shadow of sadness darkened her face.

"Your mother, she has passed?" Serge asked. Again his keen intuition impressed her as she wondered if all her emotions were so transparent.

"Yes, when I was fifteen," she answered. "My father and I became very close, but he died after a battle with colon cancer, two years ago."

"That must have been tough," Serge responded. "I never knew my father. He was killed in Vietnam. My American mother left me with his parents when I was four. They raised me in the village Breil sur Roya in the Alps of southern France. You would love it there. Ancient olive trees grow on terraces built centuries ago. When the breeze stirs, the leaves flutter a silvery green. I used to climb the twisted trees to pick and eat the ripe olives. My friends and I would swim in a stream fed by melting snow, so cold, so invigorating. During the summer, we would hike to the high peaks and camp.

We'd take tins of sardines, loaves of bread, and cheese. We'd catch mountain trout and cook them on an open fire. Once I came around a curve on the trail and stood face to face with a mountain goat whose eyes were as blue as the alpine lakes."

"It sounds wonderful," Teresa said.

"I'll never forget—we found a cave with shells from World War II. My grandfather served in the French army and identified the ones we brought home. He was something of a military war hero, in fact. When an enemy shell whistled overhead, he threw his commanding officer to the ground and sheltered him with his own body. He took over twenty pieces of shrapnel throughout his body. The government awarded him the Legion of Honor, the highest military medal in France."

"I saw the Legion of Honor Museum next to Musée d'Orsay," Teresa said.

"His name is there, *Capitaine* Maurice Gervais. He left his medal to me when he died. My grandmother went to live in a home for the elderly in Nice, and I came to Paris to find work."

"Is she there now?" Teresa asked.

"No. Two months ago I took the *train à grande vitesse* to the Côte d'Azur hoping to surprise her. I purchased a bouquet of roses at the flower market, but when I went to her home, the neighbor told me that she had passed away suddenly a week earlier. She didn't know how to contact me. According to her wishes, my grandmother was cremated, and her ashes were scattered on the sea. I took the roses down to the Bay of Angels and tossed them into the sea one by one."

"How terrible for you," Teresa replied, moved with

compassion. "Then you have no one."

"Somewhere I may have a mother. I suspect she returned to America to find work."

*But why would she leave you?* Teresa wanted to say but held her tongue. She did not want to hurt Serge's feelings.

"I inherited the house in Breil and rent it out in the winter to skiers, in the summer to tourists, many are Italians or Germans. I return there in the summer whenever I can."

"My parents didn't own their home, and my father had huge medical expenses. He did send me to college." She yawned in spite of herself.

"I think maybe you need more rest," Serge observed, taking her empty plate and fork.

"Decongestants always make me sleepy," she replied.

"Then *bonne nuit, petite oiseau,* my little bird."

"Little bird?"

That's what you remind me of," he explained. "So petite. A little bird."

"*Bon soir,*" she answered. *Bird indeed.*

He left quietly, and Teresa dozed until her cell phone rang. She opened it and said, "*Bonjour.*"

"Where the hell are you?"

She had not realized that the international chip in the phone would allow Alex to call directly without the country code. She hit the button on the phone that turned it off. *I'll find a new provider tomorrow and get a different number.*

\*\*\*\*

Serge looked up from the computer to serve a young French couple with a small boy. The impish smile of the small child caused a moment of pain and longing, but he directed his attention to the parents.

"We're here from Nice and did not make reservations, but we hope you have a vacancy," the husband said in rapid French.

"Oui, there is a room with two double beds on the second floor."

"We'll take it. My name is René Chambeau. Here's my credit card."

As Serge processed the room transaction, Teresa disembarked from the elevator. "I hope you feel better today."

"Yes, much better. Thank you." She crossed to the dining room where the breakfast buffet waited. She selected two bananas, Nutella crepes, and two lattes. Balancing them on a tray, she returned to her cozy room.

Serge gave the credit card to its owner and handed him an automated key. He watched the small, animated boy with mischievous eyes grin at him. Having a child had to make life more fulfilling. Serge took a bonbon from behind the counter and gave it to him.

"*Merci beaucoup!*" the child chirped.

"My grandmother lived in Nice," Serge told the parents. "It's a beautiful city."

"We like it," the husband said.

\*\*\*\*

Upstairs Teresa felt well enough to tackle the budget for the courtyard renovations. Thinking that perhaps Annette could assist her, she dialed the cell number that had been given to her.

"It's your turn to come here for coffee," she said. "Room 535."

"I'll be there in thirty minutes," Annette said.

While she waited for Annette, Teresa took the elevator down to the lobby.

Annette soon appeared outside the glass door, and Teresa ushered her inside. Her friend looked attractive in her maternity top and jeans, a colorful scarf wrapped fashionably around her slender neck.

"How did you know? Nutella crepes are my favorite," Annette enthused. "I'm taking natal vitamins now the size of horse pills." From her purse, she removed one from a prescription bottle to prove her point. Throwing her head back, she washed it down with a sip of coffee.

Teresa explained her dilemma with the courtyard.

"I'm not sure what anything costs here. I have an idea of what the price is in America but not in Paris."

"There is a flower market and paint shop down the street. We can go look.'

"Let's take the bus. It will be warmer. I had a bug yesterday."

"A bug?" Annette looked puzzled.

"I was sick, ill, *malade*," Teresa explained.

"That's a strange expression—a bug."

"Yes. I guess it is," Teresa mused as she bundled up in winter garb.

The bus dropped them off at a corner near the Seine where glassed-in flower shops adorned the sidewalk. Inside one, the temperature was hothouse warm. Annette located a fountain with an electric pump that recycled the water around through a hose while Teresa examined red, pink, and white begonias.

"Begonias will root themselves if you pinch off stems and put them in water with growth stimulation hormones. By spring, I could have many plants from just a few," Teresa explained to her new friend.

"You must have some lavender," Annette said, noting the seeds. "The fragrance is so wonderful and so quintessentially French."

They jotted down prices and made comparisons with other shops. Next they gathered cards with various paint colors and prices.

"What do you think is a fair price for the labor?" Teresa asked.

"No less than twenty-five Euros an hour," Annette answered authoritatively. "When you finish, I might have you do a mural for the nursery—once we find out if it's a boy or a girl."

"Teresa, Teresa Worthington? Is it really you?" A woman with auburn hair and dark rimmed glasses approached them. She wore a navy suit with a white silk blouse set off by a single strand of pearls, her appearance quite professional. "Whatever are you doing in Paris?"

"Oh, no," Teresa murmured under her breath. Aloud she said, "Ann, how are you?"

"I'm here on business. The bank sent me over to check out some possible investments. I'm on a lunch break." She studied Annette momentarily, and Teresa introduced them.

"Alex has been asking everyone about you," Ann continued.

"Things are over between me and Alex, and I'd appreciate it if you didn't bring him up."

"A lovers' quarrel?" Ann commented. She removed a mauve-colored lipstick from her designer handbag and refreshed the color of her lips. "Far be it from me to interfere in affairs of the heart."

Teresa stated vaguely that she was working on her art and thought that Paris would be very inspirational.

"I guess spontaneity is what one should expect from artistic types," Ann commented to Annette. "As far as I know, she didn't tell any of her friends she planned to leave."

*I didn't think it was any of their business.* Teresa clenched her teeth to control her rising anger. She'd never considered Ann a close friend, rather more of an acquaintance. She shrugged her shoulders.

"Good luck, then. I hope you're very successful," Ann said and wandered on.

"What was that all about?" Annette asked when Ann departed.

"It's a long story. I'll tell you over lunch." They went inside Chez Josephine, and both ordered French onion soup. It arrived with melted, gooey cheese and tasty croutons on top. Teresa related the tale of her strained relationship with Alex, his impatience, distrust, paranoia, and rage.

"Now I'm afraid Ann will spill the beans, and he'll find out where I am." Teresa cradled her head in her hands, elbows resting on the table.

"I don't know about beans," Annette said obviously puzzled by the expression, "but if she tells him where you are, you might have trouble. Would he really come to Paris, do you think?"

"He's like a bad penny. He keeps turning up. But let's get back to the budget for the courtyard." She needed this project.

Putting their heads together, they came up with an itemized estimate.

"The first florist said she would sell you the fountain at wholesale, if you agreed to buy all the plants from her," Annette reminded. Pulling a compact, solar operated calculator from her purse, Teresa tabulated the savings.

"It would be worth it."

Once she had walked Annette back to her apartment building, Teresa took everything to Serge at the hotel desk.

"Pleased to see you are feeling better," he observed.

"Thanks to your *potage au poulet*," Teresa said.

"I am off at four o'clock and would like to show you some of the sights of Paris."

Teresa hesitated.

"What is the expression you used—just friends, *les amis*?" His smile was so winning, his expression so hopeful that she said yes.

"Until then, I think I'll take a nap. I don't want to relapse."

Upstairs she set her bedside alarm clock for three thirty so she'd have time to freshen up and then dozed off into luxuriant sleep. At four, a rap at the door drew her from the mirror where she brushed her hair.

Wearing a brown suede jacket, a scarf, and leather gloves, Serge looked ready. "I thought we would tour Notre Dame. Have you been there?"

"No." Teresa slipped on her coat and a pair of royal blue wool mittens.

They took the bus down to the Seine and a boat across to the island where the ancient cathedral rose like a sand drip castle with flying buttresses and stained glass windows. Outside, a bronze statue of

Charlemagne on horseback stood upon the pavement. As they waited in the queue outside, Teresa studied the statues of the saints and apostles.

Inside Serge surprised her when he darted into one of the smaller chapels, lit two votive candles, and knelt in prayer. Then crossing himself, he arose and explained. "I always say a prayer for my grandparents."

Teresa's own Episcopal faith had faltered when her father died, but she found Serge's actions comforting. She purchased a candle of her own, knelt and prayed not only for her parents, but for protection from Alex and for a means to support herself.

Serge then took her through the church explaining various sculptures and styles of architecture. He stopped before a statue of Joan of Arc. He said he admired the innocence captured in the expression on her face. Captivated by a life-size stone crucifix, Teresa stared with dropped jaw at the suffering Christ. More accustomed to the plain Anglican crosses, she cringed at the agonizing pain of the thorns crushed upon the savior's head, of the nails penetrating his wrists and feet. Here was a man whose suffering had been more awful than her own when she had lost her parents. Totally submerged in her own thoughts, it took the squeeze of Serge's hand on her shoulder to stir her from reverie.

"To think that people worshipped here more than five hundred years ago, the same way that we worship today," he said. "There is a sense of timelessness."

Subdued, Teresa only nodded.

A crowd had gathered around a glassed box containing a crown of thorns, sharp penetrating spears about an inch in length.

"Do you think it's authentic?" Teresa questioned.

"The original crown of Christ, you mean? No, I think it's a replica brought back from the Crusades. But the original was probably very much like it."

When they exited the church, Serge produced leftover crusts of French bread from his pocket and led Teresa over to some nearby shrubs. He broke off a tiny crust and held it up in his fingers. Tiny reddish brown wrens fluttered up. One took the bread, alighting on his hand like a tamed pet. Others soon followed its example.

"You have to win the trust of little birds," he told Teresa, and she remembered his nickname for her.

"Maybe that's because little birds know all about big hungry cats," she said.

"I was right. Someone has hurt you."

"I don't want to talk about it," Teresa said sharply. An awkward silence followed. She knew Serge thought she was pushing him away, keeping him at a distance. She filled the silence. "You've been a wonderful friend."

"I respect your boundaries," Serge rallied. "Tomorrow I show your proposal to Monsieur la Salle."

To Teresa's astonishment, when they rounded the corner, a throng of skaters on in-line skates filled the street. Skaters with knee pads, elbow pads, and helmets glided down the boulevard that had been cordoned off by the police for the event. *Only in Paris.* She shook her head and then pulled her cell phone from her purse to take a picture of the happy mass. *Paris is everything I hoped it would be, and tomorrow I interview at the Rodin Museum.*

\*\*\*\*

34

The woman across the desk was impeccably groomed with a multi-colored designer scarf draped artistically around her slender neck. Her manicured nails and hair, swept up from the nape of her neck and held in place by an enamel barrette, evoked images of an expensive salon pampering. She looked self-assured and ambitious.

Intimidated didn't begin to describe how Teresa felt.

"Tell me what you know about Rodin's *Gates of Hell*," Madame Huger said. She peered through the glasses perched on her long, narrow nose.

Teresa explained the background of the commissioned work and the manner in which the twisted, tortured figures that adorned the gate represented the characters in Dante's *Divine Comedy*, adulterous lovers and other sinners doomed to eternal torment in extreme heat or extreme cold. The *Thinker* represented the poet himself and had become a famous statue in its own right.

Madame Huger did not comment. She wrote some terse notes in very feminine cursive. Similar questions followed, and Teresa felt grateful to the two professors under whom she had studied art history. She was able to answer succinctly and correctly. Finally, the interrogation ended.

"I will let you know one way or another in a few days." Madame Huger dismissed her.

"Thank you," Teresa mumbled. With sweaty palms, she arose and exited through the museum's front doors appreciating again the gorgeous mansion with its marble tiles and floor to ceiling windows. She peeked again into the room that housed *The Kiss*, a sensual tribute to the love between a man and woman. It stirred passion in her, and for a fleeting moment she thought of Serge. *I will not get romantically involved with a man again.*

The brisk return walk in the cold air cleared her mind.

Back in the hotel lobby, she told Serge, "I blew it. I know I blew it."

"You're exaggerating," he replied. "Monsieur la Salle is very favorably impressed with your proposal and wants to see you."

"Now?" Teresa panicked.

"If you need time to relax a little—"

"No, let me steel my nerves with a cup of coffee, and I'll go in."

Crossing over to the café part of the lobby, she fixed a latte and slowly sipped it. Then she braced herself for yet another interview with a stranger.

More pleasant looking than Madame Huger, Monsieur la Salle appeared rotund and jolly, a man accustomed to good food and fine wine. Dressed informally with an open neck shirt sans tie and a pullover, V-neck sweater, he appeared quite casual.

Teresa took a deep breath and exhaled slowly.

"Come in, come in," he said invitingly. "I am honored to meet such a talented young woman and beautiful, too. I can see why Serge is so anxious to assist you."

Heat flushed Teresa's cheeks and earlobes. She noticed her drawings spread out on his massive oak desk.

"You will please sit down." La Salle indicated a comfortable chair by the window.

Teresa sank down gratefully.

"Your budget seems reasonable, but there is a slight problem. You may have noticed that my hotel is not full, yes?" With his elbows resting on the desktop, Monsieur la Salle tented his fingers.

Teresa nodded inwardly dreading a rejection.

"This is our off season until the spring. But since 9/11, not as many people are traveling, and I am not sure what to expect. Therefore, I have a compromise for you. I will pay for the materials for this project. But instead of paying you to paint, I will give you a free room until spring, March $15^{th}$ to be exact. What do you say?"

Silently, Teresa considered the offer. It was not as she expected, but if she got the job at the museum, it would allow her to save money.

"Yes," she said, smiling. She felt eager to begin the project. And Monsieur la Salle liked her sketches!

"Then starting today, you will be our guest free of charge."

"I'll start working on the mural as soon as the weather turns sunny, and in early March, I'll plant the garden."

"*Très bien*," Monsieur la Salle said. "I shall look forward to its completion."

"I am so excited," she told Serge that afternoon. She had already taken chalk outside and sketched in the background along the wall. Tomorrow if the sun appeared, she'd put in the blue sky with clouds and birds in flight. Like all artists she would work from the background forward, creating the illusion of three-dimensional depth.

"You know," Serge said, after further studying the

sketches, "you should add a woman walking her poodle. Parisians love their dogs."

"That is something the French and the Americans agree upon," said Teresa.

Chapter Three

The next morning, her cell rang. For a second, fear gripped the pit of her stomach. She had changed phone providers and gotten a new number. Had Alex somehow managed to track her down?

"Hello," she said with trepidation.

"*Bonjour*," Madame Huger's secretary replied. "You have been selected for the part-time position on a trial basis. For now your hours will be nine to five on Tuesdays and Thursdays, nine to noon on Mondays, Wednesdays, and Fridays. You will give tours in English until your French improves, and sometimes you'll be expected to man the gift shop. May I tell Madame that you have accepted the position?"

"Yes, yes. Thank you so much." After closing her phone, Teresa danced around the room in jubilant abandon.

After placing the mobile phone in her purse, she dressed warmly and descended the stairs to the courtyard to paint. Serge brought her a cup of hot tea mid-morning and paused to admire her progress.

"This is the mark of a professional," Serge said. "You have all shades of blue, some yellow, and pale green in that sky. I would have painted it one solid color like a room wall. Yours looks so realistic."

"You learn a few things in art school." Her old, over-sized shirt bore an array of colorful splotches. Her hair was pulled back in a ponytail though a few wisps had escaped and framed her face.

"You have paint on your nose," he teased, wiping off a splatter of pigment. "You have been so good about sharing your art with me," he said. "It's time that you sampled some of mine. I'm going to fix you coq au vin. Starving artists must eat."

"Someone told me that Paris was a city that understood the artistic soul."

At seven o'clock that evening, Teresa showed up for the first time at Serge Gervais's apartment, a studio with a compact kitchen and a bed that folded into the wall.

Neat and clean, the room contained luscious green houseplants in terra cotta pots resting on the wide window sill. Burgundy and green Oriental area rugs added color and warmth. The bookshelves lined with interesting books, both fiction and non-fiction, indicated a wide variety of interests from travel and geography to poetry and adventure. The collection ranged from classics like Hugo's *Les Miserables,* to French translations of *New York Times* bestsellers. Perusing the shelves, Teresa could see their similar tastes in authors and subjects.

Oregano, sage, and garlic wafted through the air making her empty stomach growl.

"I'm ravenous," she confessed.

An empty green wine bottle with a lit candle adorned the table casting romantic shadows on the wall. They began with a salad of fresh greens that included dandelion leaves and different varieties of lettuce. Serge also placed before her a glass of sparkling Perrier.

"Your choice of vinaigrette or bleu cheese," he

offered.

Teresa giggled. "I had an American friend in Charleston," she explained. "She had never eaten any lettuce but iceberg. I fixed her a salad with dandelion greens and asked her what she would like on it. She picked up a leaf and said she'd normally put Weed Be Gone on it."

"So provincial," Serge said, but he chuckled at the humor. He put French bread brushed with olive oil and rosemary on her plate and then served the sauce-topped pasta and tender juicy chicken. The black olives tasted flavorful and salty.

"This is wonderful," Teresa enthused. She tried not to gobble down the food, but painting always whetted her appetite.

"I like a person who appreciates a good meal. You eat with gusto. And for dessert, we have crème brûlée." He pushed back his chair and retrieved the egg custards drizzled with caramel.

Teresa ate hers with unabashed delight savoring each delicious mouthful.

"I'll wash the dishes," she volunteered.

"We'll take care of those later. There is someone I want you to meet." He led her over to the blue velveteen sofa and clucked his teeth. From beneath the skirt emerged a beautiful cream and brown Himalayan cat. Her fur shone thick and luxuriant; her tail was a fluffy plume. She jumped up on the sofa with quiet, agile grace and sat next to Teresa.

"Cleo is shy until she gets to know you," Serge explained.

Teresa scratched the cat below her ears and under her chin and listened to deep, satisfied purring. "She's beautiful."

"And she's going to be a mother soon. How would you like one of the kittens?"

"Do you think Monsieur la Salle would allow me to keep one in my hotel room?"

"You could keep the litter box on the fire escape," Serge said.

"It would be fun to watch the antics of a kitten."

"Then you shall have the pick of the litter."

\*\*\*\*

Thursday Teresa started her work at the museum. Although the facility boasted hand-held tape recorders and headphones for self-guided tours, the staff also provided in-depth seminars by special request. Teresa trained for these presentations with three books and a CD to study at home. In the gift shop, Madame Huger taught her to use the cash register.

"You understand the euro system, don't you?" Madame Huger asked.

"Yes. And I've learned to count to a thousand in French."

She left Teresa to her job as she herself had more important matters to consider.

Few patrons visited the shop, and Teresa spent most of the afternoon pricing a new shipment of books, calendars, and posters. She enjoyed perusing the postcards of paintings by famous French artists, especially one by Renoir of a man and woman seated at a table in a beautiful garden. The man seemed to hang enthralled upon every word the woman uttered, adoration plainly displayed on his face. The artist had captured his inner thoughts in his earnest, longing expression.

Annette had invited her to supper because her husband, Guy, had to work late. Walking back to the Hotel Garibaldi after her shift ended, Teresa stopped at a *boulangerie* and picked up some pastries to take for dessert.

At the apartment, she noted Annette's thickening abdomen beneath her loose maternity top.

"I am happy to report that my morning sickness seems to be over," her friend announced. She had roasted a duck and topped it with orange sauce, *canard à l'orange*.

"Is everyone in Paris a gourmet cook?" Teresa asked. "I'm ashamed to offer anyone my specialty—shepherd's pie."

"What is it?" Annette asked.

"Mostly ground beef and mashed potatoes."

"Sounds good to me. In fact, everything sounds good to me these days. My appetite is out of control."

"You're pregnant," Teresa said. "I don't have an excuse, but I'm hungry all the time too." Teresa had started conversing with Annette in French and found her pronunciation and understanding of the language increasing daily.

"Since I discovered that you got the courtyard renovation job, I've been cultivating some herbs for you," Annette explained, as they sat down to dine. "Oh, I almost forgot to tell you—the baby is a boy—definitely. I saw the ultrasound results. I thought a Beatrix Potter, Peter Rabbit scene would be cute in the nursery."

"That would be fun," Teresa replied. "I loved those books when I was a child."

"Me too!"

After dinner, Annette showed her the extra bedroom.

"We could put the tree where Peter's momma lives with Flopsy, Mopsy, and Cottontail over here," Teresa said pointing to the corner near the window.

"And Mr. McGregor's garden over here." Annette indicated the left wall.

"Do you want the scarecrow made out of Peter's lost jacket?" Teresa asked.

"Of course, along with his dangling, missing shoes."

They laughed simultaneously.

****

The cozy warmth of Serge's flat had made Teresa slightly dissatisfied with the bare walls of her hotel room so using her employee discount, she purchased a calendar featuring the French Impressionists from the museum gift shop. She carefully disassembled the calendar and, using a putty-like adhesive that would not mar the plaster, decorated her room with Monet's *Water Lilies*, van Gogh's *Sunflowers*, Renoir's *Girl Among the Umbrellas*, and Toulouse-Lautrec's ballerinas.

She pulled a few of her colorful silk scarves from the dresser and draped them around the mirror. It made her feel as though she were claiming the room as her home to add a few personal touches.

When Serge saw it later, he heartily approved.

"I think you can add interior design to your list of talents," he said.

****

Teresa stood back from the courtyard wall mural absentmindedly chewing the wooden tip of the paintbrush. Squinting her eyes, she examined the blue sky, scattered clouds, and setting sun and smiled with approval. She could begin work on the foreground, and now the painting would get interesting. The outline of the café had been filled in with ochre, and she experimented with her palette by blending different colors for the bricks. Mixing various reds and browns, burnt sienna, vermillion, and crimson, she brushed samples upon the wall.

"This is where I cheat a little," she told Serge, who had come to observe.

Taking a brand new sponge mop, she dipped the end into a plate of paint, scraped the excess off on the rim, and then pressed the sponge to the wall. Removing it, she revealed a brick, complete with rough texture and varied shades. Repeating the procedure, she produced row upon row, then filled in the ivy green trim around the doors and windows.

Monsieur la Salle's friend who worked for *Le Monde* appeared at noon along with the staff photographer. He took candid shots of Teresa working and said an article would appear in the arts section of the paper on Saturday. It would give the Garibaldi free publicity.

"It will give you good publicity, too," Serge said. "Who knows, you may even get other jobs from the exposure."

When Monsieur la Salle visited on the weekend, Teresa held her breath and squeezed her palms together as he inspected her work. She saw only his back and couldn't judge his body language.

"I cannot believe the transformation," he exclaimed as he turned around. "You've taken an eyesore and turned it into masterpiece." In a fit of emotion, he kissed her lightly on each cheek. "We're already getting more reservations from people who read the article in *Le Monde*."

On Saturday night, several guests who came to dinner at the café commented that they'd been drawn by curiosity over the new mural touted in the newspaper.

Pleased when Serge met her at closing time on Sunday afternoon at the Rodin Museum, Teresa blushed slightly as he examined the nude statue of the man and woman entwined in *The Kiss*.

"It's very beautiful," he said, "from every angle."

They strolled down to the Eiffel Tower that twinkled like a Christmas tree against the dusky sky.

"Have you been to the top?" he asked.

"Not yet. I'm slightly afraid of heights," she admitted.

"But the view is too wonderful to miss," Serge encouraged her, and she fell into step beside him. "They erected the tower for the 1889 World Exposition. Eighteen thousand pieces that were manufactured in the workshops of Levallois-Perret. It took two hundred workmen to assemble it. Some predicted it would collapse after 280 meters, but, of course, it didn't."

"You seem to know a lot about it." They walked briskly.

"I did a project on it in school, recreated it out of balsa wood with the help of my grandfather. There are four elevators, one at each leg." Teresa recognized his attempt to distract her and allay her fear of heights.

At Champ de Mars, they crossed the avenue and the grassy lawn, looking for the shortest queue and joined those waiting at the south leg. As they stood in line, Teresa heard other visitors speaking in German, Spanish, and languages she did not recognize. She reminded herself that she now lived in one of the most cosmopolitan cities in the entire world.

"Some people think the tower looks like a gigantic streetlamp," Serge said.

Teresa looked up at the crossbars and beams reaching up to dizzying heights in the sky and watched the elevators slide up and down.

"How high to the very top of the tower?" Teresa asked.

"Three hundred and one meters," Serge said.

"What if the cable on the lift breaks?"

"We can climb the 1,710 steps if you prefer. It should only take about an hour."

"You're having fun teasing me," she scolded.

When they entered the elevator, she clung to Serge's arm in a manner that brought a smile to his face. When the lift jolted to a stop, he led her out on the first observation deck. Below them Paris twinkled like a starry sky in the dusky twilight.

Serge pointed out Montmartre with its gleaming white basilica. "We'll go there soon, and you can watch the artists who paint and show their work behind the church."

His hand brushed against hers. His fingers closed around it, and he placed it inside his jacket pocket to keep it warm.

"Now this isn't so scary, is it?"

"No," she said hesitantly. She thought she could feel the tower swaying, then chided herself for being childish. "Just to show you that I can be daring, I think we should go to the second platform."

They entered the elevator and ascended again. Teresa eased her anxiety by concentrating on Serge's explanations. Below them the Seine looked like a gray ribbon with toy boats. Serge pointed out Chartres, a hundred and twenty kilometers away.

"There are the towers of Notre-Dame, and those are Saint-Sulpice."

Teresa followed Serge's directing finger.

"There's the Observatory and that dome is the Pantheon, the Val-de-Grace."

Teresa found herself gripping the rail with white knuckles in spite of the fantastic view. She thought of some silly American movie she'd seen where someone's miniature dog accidentally took a leap from the tower. "You can see such vast distances," she marveled aloud though the fading light was beginning to limit their vision.

"It's like being at the top of the world!" Serge, obviously enthused, reminded her of a young boy. His eyes glowed with excitement, and the breeze ruffled his curls.

Several Japanese tourists clicked away with their cameras sporting zoom lenses that could focus long distances. They chatted to each other animatedly, but neither Serge nor Teresa could guess what they said.

When they had viewed the city from all directions, they descended to the ground. The ride down was not as nerve-racking for Teresa. As the sun sank below the horizon, they ambled back to the hotel where Serge began his shift, and Teresa went upstairs to read before going to bed. She lifted her hand to her nose and took in the faint scent of Serge's cologne. With that pleasant reminder of him, she drifted off to sleep.

The next morning she attacked the mural again adding an awning to the café, sidewalk tables with umbrellas, hanging plants, and windows with bottles of wine on the sills. Totally engrossed in her work, Teresa had no sense of time. The weather had warmed, and the sky remained cloudless. About eleven o'clock, Annette appeared on her balcony and called down to her.

"Would you like some lunch at noon? You know me, all I think about is food."

"I'll quit at eleven thirty and go clean up," Teresa said.

When she arrived at Annette's apartment, paint still stained her fingernails in spite of the shower.

"I have to use oil-based paint," she apologized, "so the mural will withstand the weather. It's the devil to remove."

"Don't worry about it. Sit down to your *jambon et fromage* sandwich."

"Ham and cheese. I learned that one at a restaurant," Teresa said. "I need to keep improving my French vocabulary. I'm getting tired of watching television and trying to guess what the characters in the shows are saying, but I do get a laugh out of American cowboys and Mexican banditos speaking French on television."

"Wouldn't it be nice if you could just be zapped by a magician and. poof, you would know another language?" Annette mused.

"That would be wonderful. I've always had such a difficult time with memorization."

Teresa looked out the window as she spoke and stopped suddenly. Annette followed her gaze. A burly young man with dark wavy hair and broad shoulders stood in the hotel courtyard below surveying Teresa's mural.

"He's handsome in a tough-guy sort of way," Annette remarked, but Teresa's face had become ashen.

"It's Alex. Anne must have told him she saw me. I knew she wouldn't keep quiet."

"He must have really hurt you," Annette said.

"He has a violent temper." Agitated, Teresa rose from her seat and moved away from the window.

"How did he know which hotel?" Annette wondered aloud.

"Maybe he saw the newspaper article," Teresa answered. "I never dreamed he'd follow me here."

"Go confront him," Annette advised. "Tell him to get lost, or you'll have a restraining order drawn up. I'll go with you for reinforcement."

Teresa bit her bottom lip as she considered Annette's offer. Boldness overcame indecision. A firestorm of determination rose within her, anger overcoming trepidation.

"Let's go," she agreed.

Both women donned their jackets and strode purposefully to the Garibaldi. Serge looked up as they entered the lobby. Annette said something to him in French, and he immediately followed them to the courtyard.

"What are you doing here, Alex?" Teresa asked. She attempted to keep her voice even, though it sounded shrill to her ears.

The newcomer turned to face her. "I came to bring you home. Why did you leave so suddenly?" He eyed the strangers behind her.

"I left to start a new life here, and you're not part of it. Go back to Charleston."

"You know I didn't mean anything by losing my temper, and I'm sorry," he said. "You can't throw away everything we've had together."

"I don't love you."

"Of course you do. I was there for you when your father died, when you had no one. You needed me then, and you still do." His voice rose in insistent anger.

"I believe the *mademoiselle* asked you to leave," Serge said, stepping forward.

"Who are you?" Alex tossed his head in disdain. His jaw jutted out, and his hands at his sides clenched into fists.

"I work for this establishment, and you are annoying one of our guests as well as violating her privacy." Serge's face hardened.

"Bet you'd like to have your chance at her yourself."

"Go, Alex," Teresa said. "You're embarrassing me and yourself. If you don't go, I'll call the police."

"I'm leaving," Alex snarled. His arrogant smirk reminded her of a vicious wolf baring its teeth. "This isn't finished. You'll come back to me like you always do."

He pushed past Serge and left.

Teresa nearly sank to the ground. She hated confrontations. She remembered the time Alex had actually broken her wrist and then taken her to the hospital and watched over her solicitously while the doctor set it. He had brought flowers and begged her forgiveness, genuine tears had wet his cheeks. He'd promised to change, and she'd believed him.

"I want to know if he bothers you again." Serge interrupted her train of thought. "Promise you'll tell me."

"I will," Teresa quietly agreed.

"Good for you," Annette said. "You stood up to him."

Teresa nodded, hoping her friend did not notice her trembling.

"That's the only way to handle a bully. That's what he is, you know."

"Full of bluff and intimidation," Serge added.

"You won't see him again. He'll take his wounded pride across the ocean where he can sulk alone," Annette said.

"Thank you both. I couldn't have done it without you," Teresa replied. But in the back of her mind, she wondered if it was over. Would Alex leave her alone? An ache in the pit of her stomach manifested her mounting dread.

"I'm going to head back," Annette said squeezing Teresa's hand. "Call me later."

When she'd exited the courtyard, Serge led Teresa to a table, and they sat down.

"Tell me about him," Serge said simply.

"He did help me when my father died," she began, "but he became very possessive and controlling. I came here to leave all that behind."

"Has he ever hit you?" Serge looked angry, and at first, Teresa thought he was angry with her.

"Yes," she said quietly. "He broke my wrist once. But he was always so apologetic, so abject afterwards."

"Don't make excuses for him. I hate men who intimidate women to get their way."

"Don't be angry with me."

"With you?" Serge looked hurt. "I'm not angry with you. I understand now why you're so reluctant to trust men. Did he force you to—"

"No, no. We were never intimate," Teresa answered. She looked away. "He pressured me, and when he discovered I was saving myself for my future husband, he became obsessed with marrying me."

"We'll make sure he never strikes you again," he said with quiet determination.

Chapter Four

By Valentine's Day, Teresa had completed the courtyard except for the garden. She had to wait for warmer weather to transplant the flowers. Her hotel room looked like a hothouse with multiple jars of begonia cuttings taking root in water. On Friday, February 14th, Monsieur la Salle rang up her room and asked her to meet him downstairs.

"Word of your talent is spreading," he said as she took the chair across the desk from him. "I've a friend, Monsieur Peretti, who owns a restaurant that serves Mediterranean food. He wants a mural inside with palm trees and sunny beaches."

"I'd love to do it," Teresa responded immediately.

"Here is his business card. He said it is best to call him in the mornings after nine o'clock."

Leaving his office, Teresa stopped by the front desk where an envelope was handed to her by Serge.

"*Pour vous, mademoiselle.*"

At first, Teresa thought he'd given her a valentine. The postmark on the envelope read Paris. No return address listed.

"*Merci*," she said, turning to take the lift. Once inside, she opened the letter and immediately recognized the slanted handwriting as Alex's. He insisted she was a tease and a slut always playing hard to get with him, falling for every male who came along.

She had humiliated him that day in the courtyard, and he said that if her new French "lover" should have an accident, she would regret what she had done.

*Alex is still in Paris. Why can't he leave me alone?* Upstairs she paced the room, reread the letter, and looked out at the street. Had Alex been watching her, stalking her? She had often felt uncomfortable walking alone especially at night. Should she warn Serge? Troubled thoughts twisted through her mind.

She decided that Serge must know. Forewarned was forearmed. She returned to the lobby envelope in hand.

"Was your letter a valentine from a secret admirer?" he teased.

"No." Her severe tone alarmed him. "It's a letter from Alex. Apparently, he's still in Paris, and he made some threats against you." She handed him the note.

Serge perused it and laughed. "I'm not afraid of that buffoon," he said.

"Alex has a knife collection," Teresa said, "switchblades, hunting knives, double edged daggers. I don't meant to suggest that he brought them all to Paris, but he's not to be trifled with especially if he's been drinking."

"And I have brass knuckles. But you, what protection do you have? I know where you can buy a can of—what is it you Americans call it?—pepper spray."

"It wouldn't hurt to carry some in my purse, I guess," Teresa replied.

"I'm about to finish my shift here. I'll take you, and then I have a surprise for you at my apartment."

"I'll get my coat and come back down."

After her hasty return, they walked toward the Eiffel Tower, and Serge showed her the shop where she purchased the protective spray and also a button alarm that could be attached to her key chain and set off to create a blaring siren.

"Now take your mind off Alex and relax."

"You have your brass knuckles?" Teresa asked nervously.

"I always carry them in my pocket. I pack a punch that is not easily forgotten," he assured her. As they strolled briskly to Serge's apartment, the sidewalks were crowded, and Teresa found herself scanning the other side of the street. She felt better once they had bounded three flights of stairs to Serge's third floor flat, gone inside, and bolted the door.

"Cleo has something to show you," Serge announced. "It's been my secret all week."

He led her to the kitchen where Cleo lay curled up in a basket nursing four tiny kittens. A folded, flannel blanket acted as a pillow beneath the felines.

"They're adorable," Teresa cooed. "Will she let me hold one?"

"You'd better let me," Serge said. "Cleo's a very protective mother."

He picked up one warm, mewling ball of fluff and grinned boyishly, a single dimple dotting his right cheek.

"I want you to have your pick of the litter," he said. "Of course, they can't leave their mother yet. But in a few weeks when they are weaned, you will have one of your very own."

"I like this one," Teresa said, staring into the barely open, unfocused blue eyes.

"He's a male," Serge said. "The three smaller ones are females. I had her bred with another Himalayan."

They took turns stroking the various kittens and returning them to the nervous Cleo. She would sniff each returned kitten and lick it clean. If one crawled too far from her, she'd pick it up by the back of its neck and return it to the fold.

"She's very watchful," Teresa observed.

"Most female cats are. It's the fathers who can't be trusted. Sometimes they'll kill their own offspring."

Teresa told him about her new commission, and from the bookshelf, Serge retrieved a travel book with photos of Nice: its well-known flower market, its avenue d'Anglais lined with palms, its sunny beaches and azure waters.

"This is going to be fun and challenging," Teresa said. She thumbed through the book, her arm resting against the warmth of Serge's arm. For the time being at least, Alex remained distant from her thoughts.

"I went to Nice often in the summers," Serge said. "My grandparents and I would leave the mountains in Breil early in the morning with a picnic lunch. In Nice, the water is warm and the color of lapis lazuli. My grandfather taught me how to swim, and we'd dodge about in the waves."

"The beaches in Charleston are lovely too," Teresa reminisced. "It's one of the things I miss most."

"Yes, I'd say being an only child, you were probably as spoiled as I was." Serge winked to let her know he teased.

"Of course, I expect to be waited upon hand and foot," Teresa retorted.

"Then let me see what is in the refrigerator." Serge

arose.

"You don't have to fix me anything," Teresa objected. "It should be my turn to cook."

"Why don't we compromise and handle the task together," Serge replied, and they continued their conversation.

"So which of our many esteemed and talented painters is your favorite?" he asked.

"I'm very fond of Renoir's work. He started as a more realistic portrait artist, but you can see how his style and technique changed and evolved when he encountered the Impressionists. The body language and facial expression of his subjects always seem to convey their thoughts, to tell a story."

Serge washed a plate and handed it to Teresa to dry. He enjoyed her animated enthusiasm for art.

"Of course, Monet is a favorite as well. What a prolific painter! And poor van Gogh," Teresa said sounding as though she'd known him personally. "He was Dutch, but coming to France changed his style as well. He never sold more than one masterpiece during his lifetime and never knew where he'd get his next meal, but there is such emotion in his work."

"He cut off his ear and sent it to a woman in a box," Serge said. "That's rather grotesque."

"Yes, he spent time in an asylum, but there are interesting theories now that perhaps he was unknowingly poisoning himself."

"How?"

"Artists used to make their own paints then, crushing the minerals themselves, combining them with linseed and other oils. Cadmium, the bright yellow of his sunflowers, is a poison. He may have ingested some from his hands or chewing on the end of a brush. It might have affected his mental state."

"Similar to the way mercury used in curing beaver pelts into felt seeped into the skin of hat makers," Serge said, "and so the expression 'mad as a hatter.'"

"That's fascinating."

"It's happened throughout history. The Romans used to eat and drink from vessels containing lead."

"Which artists do you enjoy most?" Teresa asked.

"I like Lautrec's ballerinas," Serge said. "I've always been an admirer of the female figure." He grinned teasingly. "Actually, I used to spend a great deal of time in dance studios."

"Were you a dancer?" Teresa asked. She was puzzled and intrigued.

He grew somber and reflective as though the topic of ballet had evoked unwelcome memories better left buried.

"No, I was not a dancer," he said in a closed and guarded fashion that ended that line of conversation.

"Looks like we're finished in here," he said with what appeared to be a forced effort at cheerfulness. He drained the dishwater, and Teresa stretched the dish towel across the rack.

"I'll walk you back to the hotel."

He helped Teresa into her coat letting his hands linger across her shoulders.

****

Four days later, Teresa awoke to the alarm clock's shrill blaring but groggily hit the snooze button and fell back asleep. She reawakened, late for work. She jumped up, dressed and bolted down the stairs to the lobby. Serge had just arrived for his shift obviously upset, his face ashen and his hair unruly. He carried a box that he set down behind the desk.

"What's wrong?" Teresa asked, as she grabbed a banana from the buffet and stuffed it in her pocket.

"I let Cleo out this morning, and when she didn't return, I searched for her. I found her on the sidewalk near the apartment. She had eaten something left there in a dish. I've taken her body to a vet."

"Someone poisoned her?" Teresa asked. She thought of Alex's threat. "Do you think—"

"A lot of people don't like cats." Serge read her mind. "It may be a coincidence. I had to bring the kittens with me."

He indicated the large cardboard box. "They'll have to be fed with a medicine dropper every few hours. The vet gave me this special formula."

"I'll take care of them this morning in my room," Teresa said, quickly deciding that she would call in and take a personal leave day from the museum. "At one o'clock, I have to start painting Annette's nursery. Oh Serge, you don't think Alex is responsible, do you?"

"There's no way to know."

"I'm so sorry."

"You have no reason to apologize."

Teresa picked up the box of mewling kittens. The can of formula and eye droppers rested in the corner. She took them up the lift to her room and placed the box in the warmest corner near the radiator. Then she called in her absence explaining that she would gladly make up the time whenever suitable. Using a manual can opener, she opened the formula and filled one of the droppers. Then she picked up one of the females.

"You poor little thing," she said, as she squeezed

the formula into the licking mouth. The warm, wriggling body both comforted and saddened her. One by one, she hand fed all four. Then they huddled up with each other in the corner of the box and slept.

At noon, she fixed a bowl of creamy asparagus soup and donned her paint splattered jeans and sweatshirt.

After returning the kittens to Serge, she walked around the corner to Annette's apartment building. Across the street beneath the elevated train station, two bums slept off a drunk. Teresa pulled the wheeled case for her brushes and paints over the bumpy sidewalk. She had purchased a copy of *Peter Rabbit* at a children's store. Annette came down to let her inside and led her up to the flat.

In the nursery, Annette turned the radio to a soft rock station and worked at the sewing machine making blue gingham curtains for the windows while Teresa drew an outline on the walls. They discussed the possibility that Alex might have been the cause of Cleo's death.

"He's neurotically jealous," Teresa explained.

"That's ridiculous. A relationship is based on trust, or there is no foundation at all," Annette replied. "Tell Serge, I'll take one of the kittens when they're weaned."

"That will be a big help," Teresa answered. "I guess he'll keep one himself to replace Cleo. What do you think of the outline?

Annette stood up and examined Teresa's sketch on the wall. "Adorable," she praised.

****

Serge walked to the veterinary clinic on rue de

61

Jean. A brown cocker spaniel and an apricot-colored poodle wagged their nubby tails as he entered the waiting room. They were friendlier than their owners who failed to look up from their respective magazine and newspaper. The unappealing odor of flea repellent lingered in the Spartan room. A wooden stand with informative brochures about heartworms, distemper, and feline leukemia stood next to a potted philodendron badly in need of water. The sagging plant expressed Serge's flagging mood.

*What kind of beast would kill an innocent animal?* Serge took a seat on the nondescript vinyl couch. An intimidated gray cat crouched in the corner of her barred carrier and eyed the dogs cautiously, hissing when they turned in her direction. Serge got up as he saw the receptionist return and approached the counter. He greeted her with friendly smile.

"I came to check the cause of death concerning my cat, Cleo."

She entered the name in the computer, her long manicured nails tapping on the keyboard.

"Yes, Monsieur Gervais. Dr. Roberts wanted to see you personally. Let me check with him."

She disappeared to speak to the doctor, then quickly returned to lead Serge back to the private office.

"Please have a seat." Roberts indicated a folding metal chair by the window. Serge sat confident that he was about to hear bad news.

"I examined the contents of your cat's stomach, and there were partially digested oleander leaves cut into small pieces and mixed with fish. Someone poisoned her deliberately."

Anger boiled inside of Serge at the injustice.

"Yes, it seems so." Dr. Roberts appeared sympathetic. "Had anyone made complaints against your cat?"

"No, she stayed inside most of the time," Serge answered though he had a good idea who might have killed her.

"I'm going to pass this information on to the Société protectrice des animaux along with your name and address in case there are similar reports of unnatural animal deaths in your area."

"Thank you. I appreciate your concern. I'll miss Cleo. But the kittens will be well taken care of thanks to the formula you gave me."

"Keep them inside, and only give them to people you trust to provide safe homes for them," Robert advised. "I can't tell you how many kittens are drowned, abandoned each year."

****

"It was poison," Serge said when Teresa returned to hotel. "Someone killed Cleo on purpose."

"Serge, I'm worried about you," Teresa said. "Why don't you see if there is an empty room here at the hotel where you can stay tonight?"

"If it is Alex, that's exactly what the bully wants. I won't give him the satisfaction. Don't worry about it."

But she did worry. Most of the night, she turned from side to side. Around two in the morning, she finally fell asleep. About three thirty, a scratching sound at the fire escape door awakened her. Through the curtain, she could see the shadowy outline of a silhouette. Picking up one of her shoes, she hurled it at the window and then called the front desk. The clamor of retreating footsteps echoed down the metal fire escape. Mustering her courage, Teresa looked out the window. A burly figure sprinted across the courtyard and climb the fence. Monsieur la Salle himself answered her call.

"Someone tried to get into my room from the fire escape!" Teresa said. "He just leapt over the courtyard wall."

"I'll call the police," Monsieur la Salle responded.

As Teresa got dressed, the lights came up in the courtyard below, and she looked out again. A gasp escaped her lips. Her mural had been ruined. Red paint had been splattered across her painting. Expletives had been written in capital letters. Grabbing her jacket, she took the lift down to the lobby and waited with Monsieur la Salle for the police to arrive.

"Did you see who it was?" the hotel owner asked.

"I couldn't see well in the dark, but it was a male, and he might have been my former boyfriend, Alex Sinclair." She explained why she had left the United States and told Monsieur la Salle about her previous confrontation with Alex.

"I didn't see him clearly enough to identify him." She regretted bringing trouble upon her gracious benefactor.

"I'm going to move you to another room," Monsieur la Salle said.

"I'll repaint the mural at no cost to you," Teresa assured him.

When the police arrived, she repeated her story to officers Gerard and Ayes.

They examined the courtyard and the alley behind the fence.

"Until something is resolved, I'm going to bring my dog, Gascon, to stay in the courtyard at night. He's a German shepherd and a good guard dog," Monsieur la Salle said.

"We found this spray can of red paint in the alley," said Officer Gerard. "We'll try to lift prints from it at the lab."

"*Merci*," the hotel owner replied. "And now, young lady, we'll move you to another room."

Teresa went upstairs, quickly packed her suitcase, and then followed la Salle to a less accessible room.

"We'll move all the plants in the morning," he said, "when housekeeping arrives."

The next day, Teresa felt so exhausted that she almost fell asleep in the museum gift shop. At dusk when her shift ended and as she walked back to the hotel, she felt as though someone followed her or lurked in the alleys up ahead. At each corner, she glanced behind. *It's just nerves.* She felt fortunate to have found such good friends in Serge and Annette. A tap on her shoulder made her jump.

"*Pardonnez-moi*," a woman apologized. "*Quel heure?*"

Teresa consulted her wristwatch, gave the woman the time, and continued down the sidewalk.

*I can't let this get to me.*

Relief flooded her when she discovered Serge behind the lobby desk feeding one of the kittens. Pulling up another chair, she lifted the male kitten and began to feed him.

He licked the formula from her finger with his rough tongue.

"The police called Monsieur la Salle while you

were out. Unfortunately, no discernable prints could be found on the paint can. Since Alex is American, Interpol may become involved."

"I've been anxious all day. I nearly jumped out of my skin just because a woman asked me the time."

"Don't let it get to you. Even if it is Alex, what can he do in the daylight? I had housekeeping transfer the plants for you. In another week, it should be safe to plant them to the garden."

Teresa could not suppress a tremendous yawn.

"You need some sleep. Go upstairs and nap," Serge said, taking the kitten from her. "You'll see, things will look better once you're well rested."

Teresa couldn't argue with him. Her eyelids drooped. Dragging herself up the stairs, she glanced out the window again and cringed at the sight of the vandalized courtyard with red paint splattered like blood across the wall. In her room, she fell asleep as soon as she lay down.

****

Serge didn't want to add to Teresa's worries, but he hated to have her out of sight.

The death of Cleo and the desecration of the courtyard had shaken him more than he'd let her know. Alex was an intimidating bully. *Or could he be something more?*

Though he'd said nothing to Teresa, Serge had found a Swiss army knife slammed into the door of his apartment holding a note that read: *I know how to cut throats with a single slash.* A jagged rip in the paper illustrated the fact.

Having turned over the note and the knife to the police, Serge decided not to frighten Teresa with the details. The police had discovered no prints on the knife other than his own. Still Serge wondered just how psychotic Alex was. Could it all be bluster, or was the man actually capable of murder?

Chapter Five

Warm, spring sunlight glided across the room from the window the next morning. The weather, while crisp, had lost winter's chill. Teresa packed up her paint supplies to begin the restaurant mural. Monsieur Peretti greeted her with a cup of coffee and led her to the main dining room where decorative wrought iron and glass tables had been pulled away from the wall. Teresa spread a drop cloth to protect the plush carpet.

"I want my customers to feel like they're on vacation at the Côte d'Azur," Monsieur Peretti explained. "Palm trees, white sand, cerulean water."

She showed him some of the photographs in Serge's travel book.

"These are perfect. I like the trees in this one, and the reflection in the water and the gentle waves in this beach scene."

"I can incorporate both in my composition," Teresa assured him.

An hour later, Peretti returned to examine her progress.

"Excellent indeed," he said. A wonderful odor wafted from the kitchen.

"What is that delicious aroma?" Teresa asked.

"Couscous. It's a spicy North African dish. You must try some. My treat."

Teresa had also noted several terrariums against the

far wall containing snails.

Following her gaze, Peretti explained. "I serve the best *escargot* in Paris. My snails are fed special savory herbs for weeks before they are cooked."

"I really know so little about your customs and cuisine," Teresa said.

"Ah, but you know how to make the art, *oui*?"

Teresa smiled at his confidence in her.

"Thank you," she said simply. "I won't keep you from your work."

"And I will not keep you from yours," Peretti said. "If you need me, I'll be in the kitchen."

Teresa continued drawing in great detail the Mediterranean scene. She even sketched in the shadows. By noon, patrons crowded into the restaurant. The clatter of cutlery and the rattle of china on waiter's trays created a cheerful cacophony.

"*Mon dieu!* That is exactly what I wanted," Peretti exclaimed when he returned. "Now you must take a break and try the couscous."

"Just let me go wash up," she said.

Teresa felt like a VIP as he escorted her to a small table with a single red rose in a crystal vase. A glass of sparkling water arrived, followed by a salad of various greens, sliced almonds, and dried cranberries. The couscous consisted of a delightful mixture of savory spices, semolina pasta, red peppers, and meats.

"This is delicious," Teresa told the waiter when he returned.

After the waiter cleared the dishes, she worked until three, and then returned to the hotel to start the restoration work on the courtyard mural.

\*\*\*\*

In March, the weather grew warmer, Teresa and Annette started strolling together when Teresa got off work. At seven and a half months and definitely showing, Annette had switched to nothing but maternity clothes. She had that expectant mother glow about her that made her complexion ethereal.

Annette knew her way around Paris and took Teresa to interesting shops and small galleries. Sometimes they stopped to watch soccer teams practice in recreation fields. Teresa learned that no one played American football and that soccer was European football.

"How did you and Guy meet?" she asked Annette on one of their long leisurely walks.

"He started working for a branch of L'Oréal in London and was promoted to the one here in Paris. I caught him staring at me in a café one day, all adorable and handsome. On my way out, I went up to his table and asked if he knew the time. A ploy, of course. One thing led to another, and we started dating."

"And now you're expecting your first child," Teresa said. "Was it strange to date an Englishman?"

"He acted so reserved at first. I wasn't sure that he really liked me. Frenchmen are much more demonstrative, but then he shared the poems he'd been writing about me. They were beautiful."

Slightly envious, Teresa wondered if she'd ever find someone to love as much as Annette loved Guy.

"You know," Annette responded, "it's probably safe to plant the herb garden now. The weatherman said we're past frost danger."

"Do you have time this afternoon? My room is full of plant seedlings."

"I have them all along my balcony and window sill as well," Annette replied.

The two women returned to their respective living quarters, gathered their supplies, and reconvened in the courtyard. Teresa worked on the flower beds and hanging pots while Annette planted the herbs in neat little rows with markers indicating each type of plant. Then she dissolved a liquid fertilizer in water and poured it over the seedlings.

"Thyme, parsley, oregano, sage, and mint," she told Teresa.

An hour later with the plants in place and the wall refurbished, the courtyard looked better than ever.

"We're a good team," Annette said, satisfied with their results. "But we need to have a little fun. I used to be a tour guide at Versailles, and I can take a guest free whenever I visit. Have you ever seen the palace?"

"No, I've never been," Teresa admitted. "I've read about it, of course."

"What are you doing Saturday?"

"Sounds like I may be going to Versailles."

"Guy will be off work so we'll use his car. I'll enjoy a pleasure trip now that I don't have morning sickness all day long," Annette said. "See you Saturday about nine o'clock."

Exhausted by a long day of work and comfortable in her secure room, Teresa ate a tomato and mayonnaise sandwich and then fell asleep.

The next morning after giving tours at the museum, she caught a bus to the Medal of Honor Museum. She needed a break, and she wanted to confirm all Serge had said about his grandfather. She paid for her ticket and picked up the English version of the visitor's guide.

Wandering through the exhibits, she admired the various gems that had been incorporated into the medals. Sapphires, amethysts, opals, emeralds, and rubies hung from ribbons. She read about the brave actions of Frenchmen who had fought with Napoleon, with WWI brigades, and with Charles de Gaulle. Exhibits included the Foreign Legion, battles in North Africa, and abroad. She discovered the heroic tale of Serge's grandfather saved for posterity, in a short paragraph among other deeds of valor from WWII.

\*\*\*\*

On Saturday morning, Annette met Teresa outside the Garibaldi in Guy's navy blue Mini Cooper. Teresa had been waiting in the lobby and recognized the car from Annette's description.

Popping into the passenger's side, she greeted her friend. "Very British," she commented.

"I wouldn't let him order the one with the Union Jack on the roof," Annette said. "It gets great mileage."

"I haven't been out of Paris since I moved here," Teresa admitted. "This will be my first excursion."

"If you like, I'll tell you some of the history while we're driving out. Versailles is about twenty kilometers southwest of Paris. The story is almost like a soap opera. In the mid-1600s, Versailles was just a small village with a hunting lodge. The Louvre in Paris housed the king and court. It was the seat of the government. Louis XIV wanted to be away from the mobs of Paris so he started an extensive renovation of the royal hunting lodge. An absolute monarch with an ego to match, he planned to keep powerful nobles at Versailles for long periods of time, to prevent them from centralizing power in their own regions."

"In America, we got away from monarchy," Teresa said.

"Well, later on, quite a few heads rolled here. Yes, the intrigues of the royals," Annette said. "They make modern *feuilletons televisés* seem tame. Anyway, Louis had married the Spanish princess Marie-Theresa. Do you like her name? He built the *grand appartement de la reine* ostensibly to honor his mother and his wife. In reality, he spent a lot more time with his intriguing mistress, Louise de La Vallière."

"Ah ha, the mistress."

"He went to war with his father-in-law, Philip IV of Spain, because the Spanish king had failed to pay his daughter's dowry. Versailles is the most opulent place you will ever visit," Annette said. "You will begin to understand the wrath of the populace against the rampant expenditures of the royalty while the masses toiled and starved."

"I know a bit about the French Revolution. *A Tale of Two Cities* has always been my favorite Charles Dickens' novel," Teresa answered. "The book bounces back and forth between London and Paris during the Reign of Terror. I'm glad that the English were able to take power from their monarchy without such horrible bloodshed."

"Yes, the guillotine took more heads than any English executioner, and I'm afraid the money Louis XVI spent helping America then contributed to his own downfall in France thirteen years later."

"I didn't realize that," Teresa answered thoughtfully.

They drove through the Ile-de-France region and soon reached the parking area filled with tour buses.

Annette parked the Mini Cooper, and they bought tickets to tour the palace and garden. Teresa stared wide-eyed at the splendor of the Italian architecture of the pink marble palace soaring above the green, manicured lawn like a fairy castle.

The tour guide took them through the War Salon and the Peace Salon giving details about the lavish furnishings, oil paintings, vases, and urns. Sunlight streamed through the magnificent ocular in the gold ceiling of the *galerie des batailles*. Ushered into the north wing, they explored the *grand appartement du roi* that had housed the king. His *salle de bain* included a sunken octagonal tub with hot and cold water. The massive curtained bed with its rich tapestries dominated the center of the chamber. The wide fireplace looked luxurious.

As they moved on through what had once been a terrace that joined the king's apartment to the queen's, *l'appartement de la reine*, Teresa felt overwhelmed by the Hall of Mirrors. Having enclosed the terrace, Louis XIV had installed 357 mirrors, many with gilded frames, decorating seventeen arches to create *la galerie des glaces* at a time when mirrors had been quite costly. Suddenly, Teresa sucked in her breath. Ahead in line, she saw someone who looked like Alex from the back.

"What's wrong?" Annette asked.

Wondering if she suffered from paranoia, Teresa kept her eyes on the man, but he rounded the corner and disappeared.

"You're ashen," Annette said.

"I thought I recognized someone."

"Alex?"

"Yes."

"It isn't likely," Annette replied. "Where?"

"In the front of the line. He's moved into the next wing."

But when they followed the tour guide into the new section, he had disappeared.

The queen's quarters were equally splendid with the children's rooms and nurseries above on the second floor. Perhaps because of her pregnancy, Annette showed particular interest in the antique cradles and children's clothes. "Louis XIV had hoped to make his wife queen of Spain to form a dual monarchy. This was his goal in the Thirty Years War that ended with the Treaty of the Pyrenees."

From the queen's apartments, they moved out to explore the carefully designed lawns and gardens created by Andre Le Notre with its Grand Canal stretching completely across the vast landscape. Teresa's artistic heart soared over the statues and fountains, sculpted bushes, rose gardens, and riotous colorful beauty.

"Can you imagine what it must have been like to live here?" Annette said. "Think of all the servants, coachmen, stablemen, gardeners, and cooks."

"It doesn't seem possible," Teresa admitted.

"Which rooms did you like the most?" Annette asked.

"The suite of seven rooms dedicated to the seven celestial bodies of the Greco-Roman pantheon," Teresa answered immediately.

"Very pagan for a so-called Catholic society. But many of the leaders in the church were self-serving hypocrites who only sought wealth, power, and the good graces of the royalty."

"Which is why religion fell in popularity with the leaders of the revolution," Teresa said.

"Yes," Annette said. "I am glad not to have lived in France during that time period."

"I wouldn't have wanted to live in London during the Blitz when Hitler came to power either," Teresa said. She still wondered how the man she had seen simply disappeared.

"History is full of man's inhumanity to man, so it's easy for me to believe that man is stained with sin," Annette replied.

"I used to attend the Episcopal Church regularly," Teresa confided. "After my parents died, I grew angry with God, but I'm slowly finding my way back."

"I believe He guides each of us along our own path," Annette said. "I don't know about you, but my legs are starting to hurt from all this walking, and I'm famished. It's past my usual lunch time, and this baby is hungry."

Teresa consulted her watch surprised to see that it was already two thirty p.m. Time had passed quickly.

"I know a small café where we stop by on the return trip to Paris," Annette said. "We'll eat there."

On the road again, the two women chatted amiably, each happy to have found a friend with similar interests. Teresa kept checking the rearview mirror and noticed that a gray Renault took all the same turns that they took.

"I think we're being followed," she warned. Annette glanced up in the mirror as well. She slowed the car.

"Let's get a look at him."

The car slowed as well maintaining a distance that

prevented identification.

When she turned into the parking lot of Café Claire, it sped up and passed the restaurant at a rapid speed. They could only determine that a male in sunglasses drove the car.

*I wonder if I'm putting my new friend into danger.* Teresa exited the car and followed Annette inside. They ordered French onion soup with gooey mozzarella cheese and croutons accompanied by fresh salads and salty loaves of French bread, but for Teresa the carefree atmosphere of the day had dissipated.

Still, she thanked Annette when her friend dropped her off in front of the Garibaldi.

"I had a wonderful time today."

"Me, too. *Salut!*"

\*\*\*\*

Serge traveled the dark and deserted street when he left the Garibaldi to return home. Passing a narrow, black alley, a raucous noise startled him before he realized a feral dog or cat had knocked over a trash can. Crossing the street, he sensed someone following stealthily behind him. He spun about but saw no one. A few dried leaves scraped across the sidewalk propelled by the wind. Still, his right hand slid into his pocket and into the apertures of the cold brass knuckles.

Entering his apartment building, he climbed the bare wooden stairs to the third floor. After flipping on the lights, his guarded defenses eased. He crossed to the kitchen cabinet, retrieved a glass and turned on the spigot filling the glass with tepid water.

He was about to drink when he spotted a piece of paper on the counter.

He read it hurriedly: *You're not listening. Unless*

*you want to end up like your cat, stay away from Teresa. This is your last warning.*

He crumpled it up in anger. The fact that Alex had entered his apartment made him seethe. It was a violation of his space and privacy. Serge checked the windows and closets along with the door to the fire escape. All were latched closed. If Alex had entered through one, how he had secured it on the way out?

Serge could have the police search for fingerprints, but if Alex had been smart enough to leave none on the knife, he'd probably worn gloves in the house. More annoyed than afraid, Serge was aggravated with Alex's cowardice and his silly games.

*I should have punched him when we were in the courtyard, and I had him right in front of me. These games of hide and seek are wearing me down. I'll have all locks changed immediately.*

Serge wanted to take action, but until he found Alex what could he do? Where could he be hiding? Even the police were unable to locate him.

\*\*\*\*

Up in her room, Teresa enjoyed the antics of the kittens that she had borrowed for the night. The male liked to climb up on the back of the chair and wait for one of the females to scoot by. Then he'd drop on top of her in a sneak attack. Teresa called him Jean-Jean since half of the men in Paris seemed to be named Jean-Paul, Jean-Michel, or Jean-Claude. The three females had been named Claudette, Sabrina, and Aimée. Serge planned to keep Sabrina to replace Cleo, and Annette had asked if she could have Aimée. They still needed to find a home for Claudette.

The kittens romped at her feet. Teresa picked up

Jean-Jean and placed him in her lap. His warm body comforted her as she stroked his soft neck and ears. His dry tongue felt like fine sandpaper as he licked her hand. Then he spotted his own tail and tried to pounce on it.

Teresa wondered if Monsieur la Salle's wife might want Claudette. She had met the plump, silver haired woman one morning at breakfast.

"Teresa." Monsieur la Salle approached her. "I want to introduce my wife, Marie. She saw your mural and wanted to know more about the artist."

"*Alors*." The woman had kissed her on each cheek. "I'm pleased to meet you at last. Such a talented young woman and pretty too." Madame la Salle smelled of lavender, and her blue eyes appeared lively. She seemed to Teresa a woman who cherished and enjoyed life.

"Claudette." Teresa pulled the female kitten up to join Jean-Jean. "I think you and Marie will be perfect together. You even have her blue eyes."

The kitten tilted her head quizzically.

Chapter Six

March 15$^{th}$ had come and gone. Teresa felt that she needed to renegotiate her lodging situation with Monsieur la Salle. Perhaps he wanted her to move due to the trouble Alex had caused. She approached his office with trepidation though the man had always been polite, pleasant, and fair with her.

"Enter, enter," he called out in answer to the rap at the office door.

"I hope I am not disturbing you," Teresa said.

"No, no. Take a seat. How can I help you?"

"Our agreement specified that I would stay here until March 15$^{th}$ free of charge," she began. "I'm employed now and can certainly pay for my room at the off season rate, but I would be hard pressed to pay on season rates. I am looking for an apartment.

"And they are very expensive, yes?"

Teresa nodded. Unconsciously, she bit down on her lower lip, a gesture she often employed when upset or worried.

"Fortunately, as you can see, we are a little busier but certainly not filled to capacity. You may stay on at the off-season rate until you find suitable accommodations.

"Thank you," Teresa said with relief. "You've been very kind."

"When I was a young man, I had a patron, a mentor

of sorts who helped me get established in the business world. I like to think that I try to give young talent the boost it deserves."

Teresa smiled. She wondered if he also considered Serge one of his protégés. She decided to save the discussion of the adoption of the kitten until another day.

****

"I must say that I missed you yesterday," Serge said when Teresa came down to breakfast. "How did you enjoy Versailles?"

"Let's just say I can't imagine one family living there even with the entire court," Teresa answered.

"I have the afternoon off and thought you might like to visit Montmartre."

"I would." Teresa smiled. "I've heard all about the Bohemian life there."

"I'll be free by one. Just meet me here in the lobby, but I'd better get back to work. I'm sure someone will be calling down to tell us the faucet is dripping or the heat is not working." He purposely omitted telling her about Alex's note. He didn't want to alarm her or make her feel guilty and responsible.

Teresa took her plate of mixed fruit and sat down at a small corner table. She'd fixed hot tea instead of coffee. Other hotel guests leisurely read the paper or consulted sightseeing maps. Afterward, she walked to a corner grocery shop and purchased a few staples to keep in her room. On the way back, she window-shopped and listened to church bells sounding. By one, she waited in the lobby for Serge.

"How do you want to go?' he asked. "Climb hundreds of steps behind the carrousel or take the

RATP tram to the top? You know it's the highest land in Paris."

"Don't think I want to climb all the stairs," Teresa replied.

They rode the *métro* to the eighteenth arrondissement, exited at Anvers station, and bought tickets for the RATP tram that ascended the Mount of Mars from the south.

"There used to be gypsum mines below," Serge said, "where some of the miners were entombed during political uprisings against the government."

At the top, they strolled to the *basilique Sacre-Coeur* with its four domed towers, one at each corner, and one larger central dome. The Romano-Byzantine church gleamed a brilliant white in the sun.

"The travertine stone exudes calcite," Serge explained. "It's like it whitewashes itself."

Teresa was not prepared for the awe-inspiring painting of Christ above the altar with his arms outstretched and a gleaming, gilded aura behind his head. She looked up at it for a long time, studying the artist's lifelike depiction of the Savior.

Once they exited, Serge showed her the *eglise de Saint-Pierre* and explained that in French, like the Aramaic Greek of the New Testament, "Peter" meant "rock or stone."

"So when Jesus said upon this rock, I will build my church, he used a play on words," Teresa responded.

"Yes."

"Interesting."

A few streets over, they wandered through *Place du Tertre* where artists showed their work under red canopies and multi-colored umbrellas. Some visitors posed for portraits as pastel artists captured them on paper. Oil paintings, acrylics, and watercolors hung on wrought iron fences and portable screens. An accordion player and two violinists played a tango on the street corner.

"Edith Pilaf once sang her songs on the streets here," Serge commented. "Did you see *La Vie en Rose*?"

"Yes. Wasn't it amazing when she sensed her boyfriend had died before she heard about his plane crash?"

Several gypsies in bright colored skirts trimmed with dangling coins sold iridescent scarves. Teresa paused to look at their wares. A swarthy, older woman with a leathery, wrinkled face studied Serge with sunken eyes.

"You must be careful," she warned him. "There is an aura of danger surrounding you."

"What type of danger?" Teresa asked the old woman.

The gypsy shook her head which was enveloped in a scarf. A few salt and pepper strands of hair escaped confinement on either side.

"That I cannot say without a reading."

Serge pulled Teresa along. "Don't listen to her," he said. "She just wants to make a little extra cash by reading my palm and making up nonsense."

"But I've felt it myself, ever since Cleo died. I've been worried something might happen to you." She looked at him imploringly. Her fingers gently stroked his arm.

"Don't be superstitious," Serge replied. His attempt to make light of the situation failed, so he changed the subject. "Around the corner is *Espace* Dali where the artist's surrealist paintings are showcased. We'll go inside and look around to take your mind off charlatans, ESP, and imaginary powers."

Serge brought his hands up near his face and wiggled his fingers to look eerily spooky. Somewhat ashamed of appearing gullible, Teresa followed him into the art gallery.

Later, they ambled past cafés and bars where Picasso, van Gogh, Monet, and others had once whiled away the hours. Serge even took her to a small vineyard once cultivated by a convent of nuns, but the afternoon had been ruined for Teresa. She couldn't forget the dire prediction of the mysterious gypsy woman.

****

On Monday, Teresa found herself reluctant to return to work especially after she looked outside and saw that the day appeared overcast and dreary. Still, she showered, dressed, and caught the bus to the museum. The usual patrons from all over the world lined up to purchase tickets. Teresa collected fees and dispensed brochures in languages that ranged from Japanese to English to Russian.

At the end of her shift, she caught the bus back to the hotel and sat staring out the window when she spotted Serge riding his bicycle down Boulevard Garibaldi. As he crossed the intersection, a Renault ignored the *arrêt* sign and bolted across the street. Swerving to avoid collision, Serge crashed to the sidewalk, striking his head as his bike tumbled on top of him twisting his leg at an unnatural angle.

"Stop! Stop the bus!" Teresa shouted as she charged up the aisle to the front of the vehicle.

"*Arrêtez! Arrêtez!*"

"Take your seat, please!" the bus driver commanded.

"But I know that man. And he's injured."

"I'll drop you off at the next corner. Sit down for your own safety."

Good to his word, the driver stopped at the intersection. Teresa jumped off and sprinted back to the accident. The Renault had not even paused. Two storeowners and several pedestrians had formed a semicircle around Serge. Teresa pushed through them.

"Has an ambulance been called?" She panted from exertion, put her hands against her slightly bent knees, and fought to catch her breath.

"Yes. They should arrive momentarily," said a man who stood in the doorway of a green grocery.

Perspiration covered Serge's brow, and his complexion was as pale as a corpse.

Someone had moved the bent bicycle to lean against the storefront.

"My leg," he moaned.

An abrasion across his forehead oozed blood that dripped down his temple. Teresa took a tissue from her purse and dabbed the wound. The blare of a siren split the air, and an ambulance rounded the corner its lights flashing. It screeched to a halt at the curb, and two EMTs jumped out.

Serge moaned. The male EMT lifted each of his eyelids and examined his pupils with a tiny flashlight checking for signs of concussion.

"Does anyone know his name?" the other one asked.

"Serge Gervais," Teresa answered. "He works at

the Garibaldi Hotel."

"I'm Marie Roubideaux." The sturdy woman in white scrubs stood self-possessed and calm apparently accustomed to emergency situations on a daily basis. "We'll transport him to All Saints Hospital."

As Marie and her co-worker, Gilbert, a hefty man of few words, rolled the patient onto their stretcher, Serge yelled out in pain but quickly sank back into a hazy twilight.

Teresa winced at his suffering and felt sick to her stomach.

"Is there a next of kin we should contact?"

"No," Teresa answered. "But I'm his friend. Can I ride with you?" She swallowed hard to fight her rising nausea. The EMTs conferred with each other in low voices and then nodded.

"Monsieur Bowen?" Marie scoured the circle, not sure whom she addressed.

"*Oui*." The green grocer identified himself.

"You mentioned on the phone that a speeding car contributed to the accident. Did you get a license plate number?"

"No, I'm sorry." The balding storeowner wrung his hands as though upset that he could offer no details. "I was inside waiting on customers."

"Did anyone notice the plates?"

"It all happened so fast," one female spectator answered as if apologizing.

"I saw a charcoal gray Renault," Teresa offered. "I saw it from the bus window. It looked as if the driver veered toward him on purpose."

"Only one person occupied the car, the driver," said Monsieur Bowen. "He had dark hair and wore sunglasses. I called the *poste de police*. When they arrive, I'll make the report."

Teresa scribbled her cell phone number onto a scrap of paper from her purse.

"Please tell them to call me," she said. "This may be related to an incident of vandalism. I'm not sure." She handed Monsieur Bowen the paper.

The EMTs loaded Serge into the back of the ambulance. Teresa crossed around to the passenger's seat next to the driver. She clutched the armrest with white fingers as they sped through the streets, darting in and out of traffic. With a screech of the brakes, they pulled up to the emergency room of All Saints Hospital.

She brusquely followed the EMTs as they wheeled Serge into an examining room.

"I need you to fill out some papers." A nurse handed Teresa a clipboard with various forms. Teresa filled them out to the best of her knowledge while an orderly wheeled Serge from the room. She had to consult Monsieur la Salle on the cell phone to acquire some of the information.

Thirty minutes later, Serge, who was more alert, returned to the examination room.

The nurse shined a light into each eye separately.

"His pupils are reacting well. But we'll continue to check for signs of concussion."

A doctor, Joseph Dorette, explained that the x-ray showed both the tibia and fibula in Serge's right leg were fractured. But the CT scan had ruled out subarachnoid hemorrhage. He put Serge in a knee-to-ankle cast till the bones mended. Teresa stayed by Serge's side to bring him water and arrange his pillows. He was eventually moved to the orthopedic floor to share a room with an elderly man recovering from knee replacement surgery.

"You look exhausted," Serge said. "I'll be fine. Go find yourself something to eat and take a taxi back to the Garibaldi."

"Serge, did you get a good look at the driver?" Teresa asked. She rubbed her forehead with her right hand trying to ease a throbbing headache.

"Not really. I was too busy trying to avoid collision."

"What if it was Alex?"

"Do you think he would really take the chance?"

"I don't know."

"If it was Alex," Serge said thoughtfully, "then he drove a rented car. The police could check into it."

"Of course!" Teresa said. "They can check the rental car businesses in the area."

"Promise me you'll go get something to eat first. You look exhausted," Serge replied.

"I promise."

"Oh, the key to my apartment is in my pants pocket over there. Can you look after the kittens?" He indicated where his trousers were thrown over a chair.

Teresa retrieved the pants and fished out the key.

"I'll make sure they are well fed."

She took the lift to the hospital cafeteria, went through the line and selected a pasta salad. The food revived her.

When she dialed the *poste de police* on her cell phone, she asked to be put through to Inspector Jules Gerard, the young detective who had investigated the courtyard vandalism. She told him about the threatening letter, the gray Renault, and repeated her past history with Alex. "If it is Alex, the car would have been a rental or perhaps stolen. We'll check out those possibilities. Do you know the model and year of the car?"

"No, I'm sorry." She sighed, frustrated by her lack of helpful information.

"Do you have a photograph of Mr. Sinclair?" Gerard asked.

"No, I didn't bring any with me, but I think I could make a fairly good sketch of him," she volunteered.

"Good, when you finish, fax it to this office." He gave her the number.

Taking her sketch pad from her tote bag, Teresa worked feverishly delineating Alex's wavy dark hair, his broad forehead, and straight Roman nose. His high cheekbones and squared jaw gave him a perpetually belligerent appearance. She created an accurate likeness. At the bottom of the sheet, she filled in details: height, five foot ten; weight 160; age, twenty-seven. One of the cafeteria workers allowed her to use the fax machine in the office.

In front of the hospital, Teresa flagged a taxi. After a quick stop at Serge's apartment to retrieve the kittens, she returned to the hotel. The kittens were agitated and obviously hungry. Old enough now to eat soft food, Teresa took them upstairs to feed them in her room. Once they had quieted down and fallen asleep atop one another in a corner of the box, she called Annette and related all that had happened.

"If Alex is behind this, I hope he gets arrested," Annette said.

Teresa called in to request an absence from work the next morning and arrived at the hospital before nine thirty. Serge sat up in bed and greeted her.

"How are you?" Teresa asked solicitously.

"Other than a headache, I seem to be okay. The doctor says I'll be in the cast for eight weeks, but a physical therapist is coming to help me learn to get around with crutches and a wheelchair this afternoon. If everything checks out, I'll be sent home tomorrow. I've already talked to Monsieur la Salle, and he is moving a cot to the downstairs office. That way I don't have to go up and down stairs at the apartment or worry about transportation back and forth to work."

"I can't help feeling this is my fault," Teresa said.

"That's why I'm going to let you make up for it by bringing me breakfast in bed every morning," Serge teased. A huge grin widened across his face. He reached out and took her hand in his.

"Your babies are fine. Annette is taking the runt to her apartment."

A woman in a striped uniform entered with a breakfast tray. She set it on the table next to Serge, opened a container of orange juice and poured it into a cup. The tray contained scrambled eggs and bacon, a croissant and jam. Serge ate every bit with great relish.

At eleven o'clock, the physical therapist arrived. A perky young woman with sparkling blue eyes and a pixie haircut, she literally bounced into the room on the toes of her tennis shoes before helping Serge swing both legs to the edge of the bed. She chatted with him in French and said something that made him laugh.

Teresa was surprised to find herself feeling slightly jealous. As the PT balanced the crutches under Serge's armpits, Teresa took a seat by the window feeling rather useless. With effort, Serge rose from the bed using his good leg.

"*Très bien*," the PT, who wore a name badge that read Babette, encouraged him. "Now try to make it across the room."

Grunting, Serge swung his body and landed on his good foot. With strenuous effort, he made it to the window and back again. Teresa had the distinct impression that he was showing off for Babette who babbled animated praise. She must have said something about Serge's strong arm muscles because she squeezed his upper arm. She led Serge out into the corridor where he made his way to the nurses' station and back.

"Good job," Babette said. "Now back in bed. I'll return this afternoon."

"She's very friendly," Teresa noted after the PT's departure.

"French women are very warm and open," Serge remarked.

*Was that a complaint against non-French women,* Teresa wondered.

"Don't tell me my little bird is jealous?" Serge's eyes were smiling.

"Don't be silly. Is there anything I can get for you?"

"I would love a soda if you've seen a machine anywhere." He gave her some change from the drawer in the bedside table.

"There's one down in the lobby. I'll be right back," Teresa said. On the lift, her mobile rang. Inspector Gerard greeted her. "I wanted to let you know that twelve gray Renaults were checked out yesterday from various car rental companies in Paris. None of them were rented to an Alex Sinclair."

"Maybe he used another name," Teresa suggested.

"That's possible. We're certainly not ruling that out. The company located in the closest proximity to Garibaldi Boulevard did rent a car to a Brian Wedgeworth who was English. We're trying to track him down. He paid cash for the use of the car for a day."

"That may be him," Teresa said.

"As I said, we'll continue to keep you informed. If you think of anything that might be helpful, please call in. The fax you sent, is it a good likeness?"

"Yes."

"I'll take it around to the car rental offices today."

Teresa exited the elevator and walked down the corridor to the vending machine she had noticed earlier. She prided herself on accurately inserting the proper change, pushed the correct button, and retrieved the chilled can of lemonade soda.

She wondered if Serge's accident might have nothing to do with Alex after all.

"Ah, this will take care of my headache," Serge assured her when she returned.

Popping the top, he enjoyed the soda. "How are your murals progressing?"

"The one for the restaurant is almost finished, but I've been so pressed for time. I'm afraid I won't finish the one for the nursery before the baby is born."

"Then the *petit enfant* will have the pleasure of watching an artist at work. Will you come back in the morning to help me back to the hotel?"

"Yes," Teresa promised. "If you stop flirting with the PT."

"Flirting? *Moi*? How absurd."

Chapter Seven

Back in the Garibaldi lobby, Teresa wondered if Serge would have any permanent damage or pain from his injury. *Perhaps it would have been better for him if he'd never met me.* Her reverie was interrupted by Madame la Salle.

"Teresa, *ma cherie*, I was so sorry to hear about Serge. How is he?"

"In a cast up to his knee," Teresa answered. She inhaled the French woman's lavender scent. *I bet she keeps lavender sachets in her clothes drawers.*

"He's young, and I'm sure he'll mend well."

"He's coming home from the hospital tomorrow."

"Oui, Maurice told me he's going to sleep here at the hotel. Please let me know if I can help in anyway."

"Marie, do you like cats?" Teresa ventured.

"Who doesn't like cats? My precious Mimi that I had for twenty years passed away last summer. Ask Maurice. I cried for a week. A blue Persian she was. *Alors*."

"I guess Monsieur la Salle told you about Serge's cat, Cleo."

"He did. To think that someone could poison a cat."

"Cleo had kittens, and we're still trying to find homes for them all. They're in the office now."

"I must see them." Marie brought her hands

together in delighted anticipation.

She followed Teresa to the counter where Mauricette checked out a guest. They crossed behind her and opened the office door. The four Himalayan kittens bounded across the room toward them and begged to be picked up and caressed. Teresa reached for Claudette and handed the mewling ball of fur to Marie.

"My little precious, aren't you sweet?" Marie cooed. It was love at first sight.

Teresa knew Claudette had found a home.

"*Alors*, how could I live without you?" Marie stroked her new pet.

****

As he rested against plumped pillows, Serge pushed back the hospital tray. He had polished off two scrambled eggs, a buttery croissant, and a bowl of fresh strawberries, a glass of orange juice, and a cup of milk.

Babette stuck her head in the door. She wore a powder blue sweater that set off the blue in her eyes.

"So my favorite patient is going home today." She put on an exaggeratedly sad expression to show she'd miss him.

"Yes, I have to leave before I get too accustomed to all this pampering—breakfast in bed, sponge baths by pretty nurses, people waking you in the middle of the night to ask if I need a sleeping pill.

Babette laughed and crossed the linoleum floor and sat on the edge of his bed.

"I thought perhaps you might give me a call sometime." She handed him a card with her phone number.

It took a moment for Serge to realize she wasn't

talking about outpatient physical therapy. "I genuinely appreciate everything you've done for me," he said and then hesitated. "But—"

"But—you're already interested in someone."

"Yes."

"You can't blame a girl for trying," she replied. "Take care of yourself and don't run into any more sidewalks."

****

Dressed and sitting in a wheelchair when Teresa arrived at the hospital in the morning, Serge couldn't wait to leave.

"Watch this," he said with a huge grin. With a dexterous turn of the wheels in opposite directions, he popped a wheelie cutting the chair 360 degrees in three seconds.

"You're going to be dangerous," Teresa prophesied.

"All the paperwork is signed. If you'll grab the crutches, I'm ready to check out of All Saints and check into the Hotel Garibaldi."

"Allow me," Teresa said. With the crutches secured beneath her right arm, she pushed Serge into the lift at the end of the hall and tapped the button for the ground level. At the bottom, the doors yawned lazily apart, and they entered the lobby.

She had discovered a bakery around the corner from the hospital that very morning and had ordered an apple pie, the kind her own grandmother had made. When they entered the *boulangerie*, the scent of warm apples and spicy cinnamon filled the air. The baker recognized her, nodded, and disappeared into the kitchen. Teresa pushed Serge up to a marble top table

95

with a single pink carnation in a mock crystal vase.

"What's this all about?" he questioned Teresa's mysterious smile.

The baker appeared with a slice of hot pie topped with quickly melting vanilla ice cream.

"This is fantastic," Serge said digging into the dessert and relishing every mouthful as if he were starving.

Teresa watched him with simple pleasure. "I wasn't sure you would like apple pie, but my grandmother used to make them for me as a girl."

"Ah, but I told you, my mother was American, and one thing I do remember about her is that she baked delicious apple pies," Serge explained.

"Have you ever thought about trying to find her?" Teresa asked.

"Actually, I have," he replied. "It's—she probably has a new family after all these years, and I don't know if she's ever told anyone about me."

Teresa's face softened with compassion.

"Don't feel sorry for me," Serge said quickly. "My grandparents took wonderful care of me. I lacked for nothing, especially affection."

Without warning, tears sprang to Teresa's eyes and trembled along the rims.

"I miss my parents so much. Sometimes it washes over me like a tidal wave that I'm all alone in the world."

Serge's arm went around her shoulders, and he hugged her to him. "You don't have to be alone, little bird." Teresa dabbed her eyes with a napkin.

"Sorry for the breakdown. It was two years ago on March $2^{nd}$ that my father died. I haven't been to church since then, and I used to attend every Sunday. I even sang in the choir."

"There's an American Protestant Church here in Paris where they speak English. You might feel comfortable there. But you don't have to be inside any particular building to pray. God hears you from the temple of a park or a mountain top or the humblest dwelling."

"I didn't realize you were so philosophical."

"My grandfather was a good teacher. He considered the priesthood before he met my grandmother. They raised me on the scripture and the writings of St. Francis and St. Augustine."

"My parents raised me on the *Anglican Book of Prayer* and the Bible, but somehow it didn't stick when the tragedy struck. At first, I felt numb with shock; then I grew angry. After Alex pursued me, I had another whole set of problems."

"You need a place to rest, little bird," he said and then whispered, "*Je t'adore.*"

At first, Teresa couldn't be certain she'd heard him correctly, and then she did not know how to reply.

"And you need to get to the Hotel Garibaldi," she said finally. "Monsieur la Salle has the office nicely arranged for you with a cot and a microwave." After paying the baker, she pushed the chair down the boulevard.

At the Garibaldi, she wheeled Serge out to the courtyard. The plants had begun to grow and blossom. She had added hanging baskets at each corner of the enclosure overflowing with foliage and flowers. The repairs had been completed.

"You've transformed an eyesore into an Eden,"

Serge commented. He squeezed her hand her hand affectionately, and the warmth traveled up her arm like electricity. Wheeling the chair about on his own, he maneuvered toward the office. He laughed as three playful kittens emerged from behind the lobby desk, pouncing on each other and chasing their own tails.

"Maybe you should offer one of them to the physical therapist you're so fond of," Teresa said just to gage his reaction.

"I couldn't part with even one of them," he said. "Guess I'll have to find another way to express my gratitude," he added just to needle her.

"Humph," Teresa grunted.

Straightening the crutches, he lifted himself from the wheelchair, made his way behind the front desk, and eased into the chair behind the computer.

"I can't stop thinking that if you hadn't gotten involved with me, you wouldn't be hurt right now," Teresa said.

"Getting involved with you, as you put it, has brought me lots of happiness," Serge said. "And we're not sure that the driver was Alex. We may be building a whole case against him when none in fact exists."

"I didn't realize how much you've come to mean to me until I saw you get struck by that car. For a moment, I thought—"

"You thought I died? No such luck. You're stuck with me," he teased.

"I'm glad." She smiled.

****

For several weeks, their routine continued normally. Serge divided his time between work and Teresa. March turned into April, and the police still had not brought in a suspect. One Wednesday, Teresa brought a roast beef sandwich to the front desk where Serge worked. She was about to unwrap the paper from a second sandwich that she had purchased for herself when her mobile rang.

"Teresa, Annette here. My labor has started."

"Are you okay? This is early."

"My water broke, and I've called a taxi. Guy is supposed to meet me at All Saints Hospital, but he's in Lyon on business. Please come ride with me." She groaned suddenly as another pain gripped her lower back in a vise.

"I'll come right over."

Serge raised his eyebrows as if asking for details.

"Annette is in labor. The baby's on the way."

Teresa grabbed her purse from the counter.

"Her husband's out of town. What if he doesn't get here in time?"

Serge watched her in amusement.

"I've never seen a baby born," Teresa said.

"I've helped with farm animals, kittens, and pups, but you'll have professionals at your disposal."

"What should I take?"

Serge took her hand to calm her down and looked directly into her eyes.

"She just needs someone to reassure her, and you need a glass of wine." He took a bottle from behind the counter and poured her a glass.

"But I don't drink," Teresa protested, then bolted it back like a shot.

Serge burst into laughter.

"Right," she said, letting out a deep breath. She gave Serge a peck on the cheek.

"I've got to go."

She dashed out the door and trotted around the corner. In the lobby of her apartment building, Annette pushed open the heavy glass door. She gripped a compact suitcase, in one hand, her purse in the other.

"This is three weeks early," she said. Her eyes were wide with fear.

"Everything will be fine," Teresa replied. "Maybe the doctors miscalculated the due date."

A taxi lurched up to the curb and stopped. Teresa ushered her friend inside and then slid in next to her. She rattled instructions to the driver in French, and the cab darted out into the traffic. Teresa watched Parisian drivers coming in from all directions to the multi-lane circle around the Arc de Triomphe and wondered how they avoided collisions. She cringed as the cab careened around corners and cut across lanes, but she became even more agitated as they got caught behind a lumbering double decker tour bus, and Annette cried out in pain.

"Massage my lower back," Annette commanded. "It hurts. Oh, it hurts."

Teresa rubbed her friend's back and instructed her to take deep breaths and slowly exhale. In a few minutes, the torment passed. The driver, motivated by fear of a child being delivered in his back seat, passed the tour bus and sped to the hospital. Screeching to a stop in front of the emergency room entrance, he hopped out of the cab to assist Annette while Teresa ran inside to inform the receptionist of their arrival. An orderly pushing a wheelchair retrieved Annette, and Teresa helped her fill out admittance forms. Then they were taken to the maternity floor.

Annette's anxiety abated as a nurse began to explain something to her in French.

"She's going to see if I can have an epidural for pain," Annette explained.

While the nurse was gone, Teresa helped Annette slip out of her clothes and into a hospital gown.

"I hate these things," the mother-to-be confided.

"*Très chic*," Teresa teased.

Annette's obstetrician, Dr. Rene Fayette, entered with the nurse and examined Annette. "She's dilated ten centimeters."

Annette tensed and gritted her teeth as another contraction gripped her body. Teresa winced in sympathy as the doctor inserted a needle inserted in Annette's spine to administer the pain medication. The nurse turned the radio to a station that played soothing music while Teresa held a cool, damp cloth to her friend's forehead.

When another contraction hit, Annette expressed amazement. "I could feel pressure, but no pain," she said. "It's wonderful."

"The marvels of modern medicine," Teresa replied.

"I hope Guy gets here in time. I don't want him to miss the birth of his son."

"I'm sure he's trying."

"Awww," Annette groaned. "I'm glad I didn't feel the full brunt of that one."

"I'm sorry I haven't finished the mural in the nursery yet."

"We have time. I've read that a baby's eyes don't focus well at first. They prefer black and white designs."

"What are you going to name him?"

"Jean-Paul, after my father."

"I like it, even if it sounds like a future pope," Teresa teased.

"My father is a wonderful man, and he loves children. I hope my son grows up to be like him. Aw, here comes another one."

"Push," the nurse instructed. "Push."

Teresa offered her hand and quickly regretted it as Annette squeezed her fingers in a bone-crunching grip.

"Guy is missing everything." Annette panted.

"You're going to be here a while," the doctor said. "First babies are notoriously slow."

Once the pressure had passed, Annette released Teresa's hand. Her fingers tingled.

Hours passed, and finally Guy appeared at the door disheveled and anxious.

"Guy!" Annette cried out. Instantly, he rushed to her side and gave her a quick kiss on the forehead.

"I thought the TGV would never get here. One of the fastest trains in the world, and it wasn't fast enough." He turned to Teresa. "Thank you for coming with her."

The contractions grew stronger and more frequent, and Annette became irritable and weary of the nurse repeating one more push.

"You've said that at least ten times," she complained.

"He's crowning. Let me get the doctor in here for an episiotomy." She hurried from the room her white shoes squeaking on the waxed floor.

Annette collapsed back against the pillows and closed her eyes in weariness. Dr. Fayette returned with the nurse and pulled a chair to the foot of the bed where

Annette's legs were propped in stirrups. Teresa had to look away as he made the incision. The baby came forth with the next contraction, and Teresa joined the ecstatic parents in awestruck wonder at the perfect, tiny body of the staring infant.

"He's a few weeks premature, but his color is good. He looks healthy though he probably weighs less than three kilograms," Dr. Fayette said.

"What blue eyes!" Teresa exclaimed. "He's beautiful."

Dr. Fayette handed the baby to the nurse who wrapped him in a soft blanket. She gave him to Guy whose eyes watered. He placed little Jean-Paul in his mother's arms. Annette drew back the blanket from his head and touched the downy blond fur that covered the baby's head. His hands were balled in fists as he gave an enormous yawn.

"This is the most amazing thing I've ever witnessed," she said.

Dr. Fayette gently massaged Annette's abdomen and removed the placenta. The nurse took the baby and placed him gently in a clear plastic layette.

"I think Annette will probably need some sleep," Dr. Fayette said.

Guy kissed his wife, and then he and Teresa followed the nurse to the nursery. To her great surprise, Teresa saw Serge in the hallway. Moving as quickly as he could on crutches, he came up to admire the baby.

"Isn't he beautiful," Teresa crooned. "Oh, I'm sorry. Serge, this is Annette's husband, Guy, and this is Jean-Paul."

"The delivery went well?" Serge asked. "Your wife is fine?"

"Everyone is healthy and well," Guy answered. "I feel like I'm on a high and may never come down. A son! I have a son."

Serge looked at Teresa and smiled. "He does seem a little excited, doesn't he?"

"You didn't have to come all the way down here," Teresa said. "You didn't walk, did you?"

"No, I took a cab. I didn't want you coming back alone at night, *petite oiseau.*"

It was Guy's turn to laugh.

"Little bird?" he said. "You know a Frenchmen is smitten when he starts coming up with pet names."

Teresa blushed. The nurse continued on to the nursery.

"Tell Annette I'll be by to see her tomorrow," Teresa said to Guy.

"I'll tell her, and thank you again for being here with her." He left to follow the nurse.

"I thought maybe you came by for some more physical therapy," Teresa teased Serge.

"Only if you're the one conducting it."

They walked to the elevator and rode to the lobby where they exited and hailed a cab.

## Chapter Eight

The next morning when Teresa came down to breakfast before heading off for work, Serge joined her with a cup of coffee.

"I must confess that my concern about you last night was not totally unfounded."

He took a folded paper from his back pocket and placed it on the table. "I'm not in the habit of reading other people's mail, but it wasn't even in an envelope. I found it partially jammed under the door to your room yesterday afternoon."

Teresa opened the letter and read the typed note: "I watch you every day, hidden yet in plain view. You wore the yellow blouse that I like so much yesterday, so I know you still think of me, too. Quit being obstinate, or there will be repercussions you'll regret." No signature, but Teresa remembered Alex remarking once that he liked her yellow blouse.

"Does it sound like Alex?" Serge asked.

"Yes." Teresa bit her lower lip. "Why can't he leave me alone?"

"You realize he knows exactly where your new room is and somehow he got upstairs without being seen.

Teresa shuddered involuntarily.

"I'll call Inspector Gerard when I get to work. I'll leave the letter here so he can come by and pick it up."

"I wish you'd stay here today," Serge said.

"I can't stop living. I can't just hide. I've got to work at the museum this morning, and I promised I'd add more detail to the restaurant mural this afternoon. I also want to go by the hospital later."

Serge took her hand and looked earnestly into her eyes. "Be careful," he said.

"Stay with the crowds. I'll go with you to the hospital tonight."

"What about you? He sees you as a threat. You're the one he went after last time, and now you're even more vulnerable."

"I'm armed and dangerous," Serge said, brandishing his crutch like a weapon.

Teresa shook her head in amusement. "You're so endearing," she said.

But as she emerged from the building, she watched everyone on the sidewalks.

The usual vagrants slept beneath the stairwell of the transit station. Along the boulevards, people like herself hurried to work. Several times she looked back over her shoulder. All morning with a calm façade, she gave tours of the statues in the gallery, but beneath the surface a wave of anxiety churned.

After a quick lunch, she channeled the anxiety into activity as she layered detail after detail on to the mural.

"It looks so real, so three dimensional," commented one diner, "that someone is going to walk right into it and get knocked out."

After cleaning her brushes, Teresa left, stopping briefly at a toy store to purchase a teddy bear before returning to the Garibaldi. To her relief, Serge stood behind the counter assisting a guest who was checking out. He looked up and smiled when she entered.

True to his word, he accompanied her to All Saints Hospital as soon as he finished work. Together they presented Jean-Paul with his first teddy bear.

"I'm so sorry I fell asleep on everyone yesterday," Annette apologized. "It's no wonder they call it labor. It's a lot of work."

Her guests laughed.

"When I did wake up, I devoured supper like a starving beggar."

"Our son has a healthy appetite too," Guy said.

Looking at mother and infant, Teresa wondered if she'd ever have such a beautiful child. She watched Serge take up the baby and coddle it.

"He's a natural," Guy observed aloud. "Uncle Serge."

As they strolled down the Champs Elysées afterward, Serge pulled her arm through his.

"I feel so complete with you as though I've known you a long time," he said.

"Do you believe in soul mates?"

"I didn't, but you just might convince me in time."

He stopped and studied her seriously. *He's going to kiss me*, and then she felt his lips warm upon hers, his tongue tentative and then inviting as she abandoned herself to the kiss that coursed all the way to her toes like an electric current.

"I've wanted to do that for a long time," he confessed as they drew apart.

"Serge, I—I'm not ready—"

He hushed her with a single finger placed delicately to her lips. "No expectations or demands."

They resumed their amiable stroll, her hand in his.

"I got a letter today from the property manager in Breil. The lease on my grandparent's house expires in two weeks, and there are some repairs that need to be done before it's rented again. It would be less expensive if I did them myself. I want you to see Breil."

Teresa felt panic rise within her. Alerted by her pause, Serge continued.

"There are several bedrooms in the house. You'd have your own, of course, and the doors lock." He grinned.

"Let me think about it," she said.

"The reason I want you to come is that I don't want to leave you here alone with these threatening letters. Maybe if you slipped out of town, Alex would think you'd left again and give up. Maybe he'd go home."

"When I spoke to the police today, they didn't have any new information," Teresa said.

"I know. I asked when Jules stopped by to pick up the letter."

"I'll think about it, Serge. I will."

In the distance, they saw the Eiffel Tower, a light in the darkness.

Sunday morning, Teresa awoke with a headache. She had not slept well. As much as she liked Serge, perhaps loved him, she didn't trust her own judgment.

Alex had been nice at first and then gradually grown controlling and jealous. Hadn't she come to France to establish her own independence? In the distance, she heard church bells chiming. She had wondered about the American Church Serge had mentioned.

Getting out of bed, she wandered over to her laptop and booted up the Internet. Within a few minutes on

Map Quest, she had directions to the church.

After a quick shower, she donned a dress and went down to hail a taxi. Serge knelt behind the desk on one leg feeding the kittens. The leg in the cast stretched out in front of him like he performed a Russian dance.

"You're dressed up," he said, appraising her with an approving smile.

"I've decided to visit the church you mentioned," Teresa said.

"I'd go with you if I didn't have to work," he said.

"I think I need to go alone," Teresa said. "It's been so long that the roof might cave in." She giggled nervously.

"Just be—"

"I know—careful," she finished for him.

She ate a banana and a cup of orange juice, before hailing a taxi and giving the driver directions. In a few minutes, she exited the cab and felt small and alone before the solid building. For a fleeting moment, she thought about jumping back in the cab, but a friendly couple smiled at her, and she mustered the courage to enter though she sat in the back pew.

To her surprise, no organ music played. Instead, a trio of guitarists and a drummer were ensconced on the raised dais behind the pulpit. As they began to strum "Amazing Grace," an old favorite from her childhood, two young women, an alto and a soprano, sang a duet, encouraging the congregation to join the chorus. They lifted their hands and closed their eyes as they offered up their praise to God. When they sang the last verse, Teresa felt tears streaming down her cheeks. "When we've been there ten thousand years bright shining as the sun, we've no less days to sing God's praise than when we first begun."

*Oh Momma and Daddy, if I just knew that you were safe and waiting for me somewhere.*

A voice in her head answered, *Trust me. Have faith.*

More songs of praise followed: "Oh Lord, Make Me a Sanctuary" and "It Is Well With my Soul." Teresa had never heard anything like it in her Episcopal church.

A young pastor stepped up to the pulpit and welcomed the congregation and any visitors.

"It's our hope that you will feel God's presence in the praises that we offer up."

He then asked the worshippers if anyone needed prayer and several names were called out. The congregation voiced requests for healing, comforting, and even conversion. Led by the pastor, the congregation bowed their heads and asked for forgiveness of their sins.

Teresa noticed less liturgy, fewer memorized statements blindly repeated without heartfelt conviction. When the sermon began, she felt that the minister, Reverend Richard Salley, had her strangely in mind. But how could he have known what she needed to hear?

"Our God is a God of new beginnings," he said. "He never deserts us though we may wander away from him. Sometimes we blame God when things go wrong. Why, we ask ourselves, does He allow suffering or life-changing events to turn our lives upside down? But God is the Master Artist. He plans the entire painting while we are sometime caught staring at one brush stroke, not understanding that all things work together for good if we allow Him into our lives."

When the service was over, Reverend Salley retreated to the front door to greet the members of his congregation.

"I enjoyed your sermon," Teresa told him as she exited.

"Thank you." He took her hand warmly in his. "You're visiting, aren't you? I hope you'll come again. We have all sorts of ministries here including a soup kitchen for the homeless at noon on Wednesdays and Thursdays."

"I'd like to volunteer sometimes," Teresa said. "My name is Teresa."

"It's nice to meet you. Join us anytime you'd like."

When she returned the Garibaldi, Serge teased.

"I don't see any plaster in your hair, so I guess the ceiling didn't collapse."

Teresa laughed. "No," she admitted ruefully.

"Have you thought anymore about the trip to Breil? I need to reserve train tickets," he said.

"Yes," Teresa said. "I'll go with you. But this afternoon, I need to go work on the mural for baby Jean-Paul."

They were interrupted by Monsieur la Salle strolling inside from the courtyard.

"Since the mural has been such a crowd pleaser, I've decided on another addition," he said.

Serge and Teresa turned quizzically toward each other.

"Follow me," the hotel proprietor said.

They heard the new attraction before they actually saw him.

"*Bonjour*!" a voice squawked. "*Mangez dans le*

*restaurant ce soir.*"

A brilliant cobalt blue, lime green, and lemon yellow parrot tethered to a perch turned his head sideways to examine them.

"He's fifty years old and may live to be a hundred," Monsieur la Salle informed them. "He has a vocabulary of over sixty words. But don't get too close. He might bite."

"Don't get too close. He might bite," the parrot echoed as though warning them about Monsieur la Salle. Teresa stifled a grin with her hand, but Serge laughed outright.

"What's his name?" she asked.

"Mimicry."

"That's appropriate."

"He's a macaw from Central America."

"Mimicry, Mimicry, Mimicry," the bird announced moving sideways across his perch with small steps.

"I'm sure he'll attract patrons," Serge said. "He's quite the comic."

Chapter Nine

"It's a big step," Annette said from the chair in the nursery where she sat breast-feeding Jean-Paul. The baby wrapped in a fuzzy pastel blue blanket looked cozy and content.

"We're going to have separate bedrooms," Teresa hastily explained as she painted Peter Rabbit's blue jacket.

Annette laughed. "I guess you could fight off a guy with a knee-high cast if you had to, but why would you want to discourage him? Serge is handsome, polite, and ambitious. I think you'd better snatch him up before someone else does."

"He is all those things, isn't he?" Teresa agreed. "But so was Alex when I first met him."

"Look, he's fallen asleep," Annette said. "He always does this." She modestly buttoned her cotton print blouse and moved the baby to his cradle. "When you get a chance, take a break. Guy brought home all sorts of sample cosmetics. We'll give each other make-overs. It's supposed to keep me from getting postpartum depression."

"Let me finish this one section," Teresa said. She painted a crimson lady bug onto a blade of chartreuse grass knowing that small details made her depictions more intricate and interesting.

"I'll go make us some tea," Annette replied.

Teresa finished the corner by applying some ferns and dandelions. Then she reached up with her right hand and massaged her neck and shoulders. She could use a break she decided. Putting the brushes into a large cup of water to soak, she stood up and glanced at the contented baby sleeping beneath his soft blanket. Then she joined Annette in the kitchen.

"You're wearing off on me," Annette said returning with a tray, "with this hot tea in the afternoon. Cream?"

"Please and a lump of sugar," Teresa replied.

Her friend had gotten out two hand mirrors and an array of cosmetics from eye shadows to powders to perfumes.

"I guess if I concentrate on my face, I won't think about my abdomen that shakes like jelly now," Annette said.

"It will firm up in no time," Teresa encouraged her. "Besides that handsome little boy is worth it."

They sipped their tea and then began to sort through the amazing colors of lipsticks.

"We'll put on our own foundation and powder, but then let's choose eye shadow and lipsticks for each other," Annette said.

"I've never worn many cosmetics," Teresa said.

"But you're an artist, so think of my face as a canvas and create a masterpiece."

"I don't think I can improve on all that God's already given you," Teresa said.

"Just enhance it a bit. Humor me, Teresa. For the past few months, I've felt like a blimp. I'd like to feel feminine again," Annette said as she dabbed ivory tinted foundation onto her face.

Teresa followed her lead and examined her own reflection in the hand mirror.

"You have a nice complexion," Annette said, "and fantastic cheekbones. You should accent them." She brushed a darker powder just below Teresa's cheekbones.

"This lavender eye shadow should bring out the brown in your eyes," Teresa said.

Annette studied Teresa's eyes. "Yours are green with golden specks like the golden highlights in your hair."

"My dad used to say I had cat eyes," Teresa commented. "Kitty was his nickname for me."

"That's quite the opposite of Serge's name for you," Annette replied. "Oh, this mascara is nice."

When they finished, Teresa had to admit she felt elegant.

Serge's response when she returned to the hotel was very French. "Ooh la là. *Très belle*. What is the occasion?"

"I wanted to experiment a little bit, and with the post-partum blues, Annette needed cheering up."

"I know I'm cheered up," he enthused. "We must go out to dinner. And then I have something to show you."

"Really, you—"

"No excuses. Go get dressed. Uh, I'm afraid, I'm limited to shorts with this cast."

"Then let's go back to that fabulous pizza place," Teresa said.

She took the lift to her room and was relieved that no note had been shoved under the door. Selecting a pale green sundress with spaghetti straps and a white sweater, she brushed her hair one last time and returned to the lobby.

Whatever aftershave cologne Serge wore smelled wonderfully intoxicating. As they strolled to the restaurant, he pulled her arm through his.

"I've been wondering about the note that was left for you," he said. "What do you think he meant by the phrase *hidden but in plain view*?"

"I've thought about that myself," Teresa said. "I keep a sharp look-out all the time."

"Maybe Alex is wearing a disguise."

"He could hardly dress up like a woman," Teresa said.

"Why would it have to be a woman? An older man perhaps? He could grow a beard, dye his hair."

"That's true," Teresa said. "I do often feel like someone is watching me. I keep hoping that since the police are looking for him, he'll give up and go away."

"In my experience problems rarely just go away," Serge noted. "If wishful thinking solved all our problems, life would certainly be much simpler."

As they rounded the corner and reached the front step of Felippe's, Serge said, "Watch this." He swung back on the crutches and landed with his good leg on the top of the step.

"You're getting quite good with those." Teresa slid into an empty booth.

The pizza arrived just as Teresa remembered it—gooey and delectable. She smiled at Serge.

"After dinner, we're going to the building where I plan to start my restaurant, Chez Gervais. I must warn you, it doesn't look like much now, which is why the rent is so reasonable. But once it's decorated, well, I'm hoping that you'll help me with that."

"Then you're almost ready to open your business? I'm so excited for you."

"If I make the necessary improvements to my grandparents' house and increase the rent seventy-five euros a month, I'm going to take the plunge."

"Yes, about your trip to Breil. I told you that I'd go with you, but I'll pay my own travel expenses."

"You will not. You're my guest. And I'm so glad you agreed. I feel much better knowing that you'll be out of Paris for a while."

They took public transit to the seventh arrondissement to rue de Jean, a narrow alley where the building that had once been a Thai restaurant stood vacant. The light from the street lamp illuminated the interior. Shading her eyes with her hands to cut down glare, Teresa peered inside. Peeling strips of wallpaper drooped from the walls. A cracked mirror hung behind a dusty bar.

"I know it looks like a disaster, but imagine black and white tile floors, white linen table cloths with black napkins, crystal goblets with flickering candles," Serge said. "A single red rose at each table."

"It will be lovely, quaint and romantic."

"Romantic, yes," he said, his lips moving closer to hers. When they met her own, Teresa breathed in the heady smell of his cologne. Their lips lingered, and the kiss intensified. Warmth rose up her spine where Serge's hand rested on the small of her back. Her skin tingled. She wound her fingers through the soft hair at the nape of his neck. It took self-control to pull herself gently away. She had never felt the same love for any other man.

"Let's walk along the Seine," Serge suggested, leading her several blocks away.

"Some of the cafes have outdoor dining with musicians. Not that I'll be dancing with these." He indicated his crutches. "*Alors*. It's too bad you know. I'm quite good at the tango."

"I prefer the waltz," Teresa replied. "My parents enrolled me in ballroom classes."

"No, the Latin dances are much bolder, bodies taut, moving together as one, thigh to thigh, hip to hip."

The glittering lights of the boats motoring the river reflected in the water.

The passengers chatted gaily. Accordion music stirred the air with a dramatic tango as couples spilled out of the restaurants and danced on the sidewalks.

"Why do the partners always look so angry with each other in the tango?"

"It's the tension, the passion, the game of amour."

"I'd think you had too much wine at dinner," Teresa teased, "if I didn't know you drank water."

"I think I'm intoxicated by you," Serge said. "Do you know how long it's been since I've felt this way? I've been so focused on opening the restaurant, working and saving. I haven't allowed myself to date."

Teresa said nothing.

"I know you're distrustful, but don't judge all men by one man's behavior."

The tango music subsided, and the musicians struck up a slow waltz.

"Now this is just a box step," Serge said. "Put your arms around my neck."

Tentatively, Teresa did. He swayed on the crutches in rhythm with the music, his mouth close to her ear, he whispered, "I can see how you like the waltz."

Above them, the crescent moon shone down, and stars sprinkled the heavens. Teresa felt that Serge's arms were just where she belonged.

"What is the cologne you're wearing?" she asked.

"Do you like it?"

"Yes."

"It's Mont Blanc, named after the highest mountain in the French Alps."

"No wonder it's so heady."

He laughed softly in her ear. Suddenly, a cold shiver gripped Teresa. She turned around certain that someone menacing watched them.

"Let's take a taxi back to the hotel," she said, trying to keep the fear out of her voice, but she didn't fool Serge.

"What's wrong?" He looked up. "Did you see him?"

"No," she answered hesitantly. "But I have a funny feeling."

"I'll hail a cab." He turned to leave.

"No! Don't go alone. Let's use a phone," she said, taking out her mobile.

After making the call, they climbed the steps to the street above. A variety of vendors' booths sold small models of the Eiffel Tower, postcards, scarves, calendars with paintings by Monet and van Gogh, and other souvenirs.

"Oh, no," Serge said. "Avoid the gypsies."

But before he could explain, a swarthy woman bedecked in a colorful skirt and dangling earrings took Teresa's hand.

"I'll give you a free reading," she said. "There is a

dark aura surrounding you."

She turned Teresa's hand palm up and traced the lines that ran down it. As she seemed to fall into a trance, spectators gathered.

"I see an ebony raven with eyes of piercing scarlet. His wing span is extensive and casts a deep shadow. There is a grave threat to your life," she announced with practiced drama.

The crowd that had formed a ring around them emitted gasps and whispers. With firm authority, Serge took Teresa's hand. His eyes snapped like newly lit dried kindling.

"Our taxi has arrived," he said, dragging Teresa away.

"Don't listen to a word she said," he warned as they tumbled into the rear seat of the cab. "She's just drumming up business with a show. Call it false advertising. Superstitious drama."

"I'm not completely naïve," Teresa replied, though she had to admit if only to herself that her heart pounded abnormally in her chest. The gypsy's fingers had been ice cold like those of a corpse. It wasn't until they pulled up in front of the hotel that she grew more at ease.

"A holiday is exactly what I need," she said with conviction as she alit from the cab. "We leave in two weeks?"

"Yes," Serge replied. "In two weeks."

"It can't come soon enough. But you know that does give me time."

"Time for what?"

"In America, we have showers for new babies where people are invited and bring gifts for the newborn. Perhaps Monsieur la Salle would let us have a shower for Annette and Guy in the courtyard."

"He probably wouldn't mind," Serge replied.

"I'll get the names of some of the couples who work with Guy, and we can have light finger food— nothing elaborate."

"You're pretty excited about this baby, aren't you?"

"He's so tiny, four pounds, six ounces."

"I like the way he grabs your finger when you reach out to him," Serge answered.

He seemed unusually serious, even a bit down, so unlike his usual jolly self.

"Is something wrong?" Teresa asked.

"No, I was remembering something that happened a long time ago. Let's go ask Monsieur la Salle about your shower idea."

The older Frenchman complied happily. "It will show off our new outdoor café."

Teresa planned the event to take place in one week, and Guy sent out invitations to six couples. Monsieur la Salle and his wife were invited as well as Mauricette, Serge, and herself.

\*\*\*\*

On Wednesday at 11:00 a.m., Teresa decided to work at the American Church soup kitchen. When she entered the building, other volunteers along with Reverend Salley were chopping carrots, onions, celery, and potatoes to add to the beef stock simmering in two large pots on the stove in the church kitchen.

"Teresa, I'm glad you've joined us," the minister said. "Let me introduce to everyone. This is Jean-Claude and his brother Pierre."

The two men were identical twins probably in their forties with salt and pepper hair. The only difference in their appearances other than clothes was Pierre's moustache.

They nodded to Teresa and smiled.

"Stephen and Yvette are our mainstay. They're a retired couple who run our facility here."

"We're pleased to have you join us," Yvette said wiping her hands on her apron and handing Teresa a similar protective garment.

"This is Gigi." Salley referred to a young woman in her twenties with bright red hair and the most magnificent emerald eyes Teresa had ever seen. She wore a necklace with a simple silver cross around her neck and smiled warmly.

"And this is my wife, Catharine." The pride and adoration in Reverend Salley's eyes were obvious. Like Teresa, Catharine had honey-colored hair that fell to her shoulders and a sprinkle of freckles than fanned across her tiny, rabbit-like nose.

"I've seen you before somewhere," Catharine said.

"She had a remarkable memory for faces," Reverend Salley explained.

Teresa could not recall their having met before. She shrugged her shoulders. "I'm American. I've only been in Paris a few months," she said. "So how can I help?"

"Follow me."

Yvette led her to a counter by the oven where dough waited in a stainless steel mixing bowl.

"We're making biscuits to go with the soup," she said as she pulled the dough from the container and dusted it with sifted flour. She opened a drawer and handed

Teresa a round biscuit cutter and then used a wooden rolling pin to flatten the dough.

Teresa pressed the cutter into the pliable mixture. They worked well together. Whenever they'd filled a pan with biscuits, they transferred it to the preheated oven and started again. Soon the delicious aroma of fresh bread and bubbling soup filled the kitchen.

"I know where I saw you," Catharine said suddenly. "You were in the newspaper. You painted a mural for the Garibaldi Hotel."

"Yes," Teresa replied. "I can't believe you remember that."

"You're very talented."

"Thank you." Teresa always felt self-conscious when she received praise and never knew how to respond.

"We'll plan to come see it in person," Reverend Salley said. "About lunch today, I feel that I need to explain that some of our guests suffer from mental illness. They're not dangerous, but they're rarely able to hold jobs for long. Unfortunately, there are not enough government-run programs to help them. If they say things that don't make sense, that is why."

"Yes, there's poor Adelle who had been waiting for an uncle who is coming to get her for weeks, probably years," Yvette said.

"Some have problems with alcohol and drug addiction," Catharine said.

"I understand," Teresa said.

The homeless began arriving at noon and waited outside until Reverend Salley gave thanks to God for the food and the company. Then they shuffled in single file in various forms of dishevelment, with wrinkled, soiled clothes, and tousled hair. Many of the men needed to shave. Teresa tried to ignore the odor of human sweat and neglected hygiene. She ladled soup into bowls and placed them on trays. An older man wearing a black beret thanked her, his smile revealed a missing front tooth. The rest were stained. A woman who had lost one lens from her eyeglasses stared at her with one eye magnified and the other squinting.

"Good morning, Adelle," Yvette greeted a woman whose ankles looked painfully swollen.

*So many needy people.*

"Extra salt and pepper if you please," Adelle sang out. "You know I like my soup spicy."

Yvette sprinkled the requested seasonings over Adelle's bowl, and the line continued moving. When everyone was seated at long tables in the fellowship hall, Teresa counted the guests in her head, seventy-six in all. As they finished their meals, she began to bus trays and bowls back to the sink where Jean-Claude and Pierre washed dishes. She listened to the conversations of some of the guests and grew particularly interested in something she overheard Adelle say.

"He bragged that he ran down a man with his car," the myopic woman told the man next to her who slurped his soup from his spoon. He barely listened, but Adelle had captured Teresa's complete attention.

"Who said this, Adelle?" she asked.

"I don't know his name, but he said next time he'd kill him."

"Where did you see this man?"

"In the Tuileries garden."

"Did he say anything else? Did he tell you where

he was staying?"

"No. He didn't speak French, and he was surprised that I understood English. My mother was English, from Yorkshire she was."

"Can you describe this man?"

"Husky, sort of barrel-chested. Dark hair and eyes. He looked mean."

"Would you be willing to talk to the police about him?"

At the mention of the police, Adelle bristled.

"No, I don't want to be involved with the police. They might lock me up again. That man might get angry. He might cut me with his knife."

"He had a knife?" Teresa asked.

"More than one. He practiced throwing them at a tree trunk. I don't want nothing to do with that man." Adelle wrung her hands with mounting anxiety, and Teresa could tell that her questions bothered her.

"No," Teresa said soothingly. "You stay away from that man, and he'll stay away from you."

On her walk back to the hotel, she wondered if Adelle had really met Alex. She was glad that Serge no longer spent the nights alone in his apartment. Leaving Paris would be safer for them both. She called the Paris police and passed on the information she'd heard from Adelle, but she did not tell Serge. Afraid that he might try to hunt Alex down on his own, she omitted the story when she told him about her day at the soup kitchen.

"There were so many needy people," she told him and described Adelle and some of the other guests.

"The next time you go, I'll go with you," Serge promised.

\*\*\*\*

Planning the baby shower helped ease Teresa's mind. She bought teddy bears to decorate the tables and made party favors that looked like pacifiers out of Life Savers, jelly beans, and pipe cleaners.

The day of the shower dawned clear and sunny. Pink, white, and red begonias bloomed in the warm beds, and the courtyard looked wonderful. Pineapple punch and cupcakes with light blue icing added color to the serving table.

Annette unwrapped package after package of adorable children's clothes: onesies, overalls, smocked tops with matching shorts. Marie la Salle ooh-ed and ah-ed over each tiny outfit and kept a list of the items and the guests so that Annette could write thank-you cards.

While they ate, Mimicry cried, "Feed the bird. Feed the bird." He moved anxiously from side to side on his perch. Teresa fed him some grapes.

"I've had such a wonderful time," Annette told Teresa when the other guests had left.

"Jean-Paul will be dressed in style for months to come," Guy added.

"Thank you so much, Teresa." Annette hugged her and brushed away a few tears. "Hormones!" she excused herself.

"I had a great time too. It was a perfect way to spend my twenty-fourth birthday."

"Today's your birthday? I wish I had known," Annette said.

"I couldn't have enjoyed it more," Teresa assured her.

Later, Serge cornered her.

"Why didn't you tell me it was your anniversary?"

Annette had obviously informed him.

Though she knew better, Teresa teased him. "Anniversary? But I've never been married."

"French, for birthday," he said.

"Then what do you call an anniversary?"

Ignoring it as a rhetorical question, Serge complained, "I should have gotten you a present."

"No, your presence was present enough."

****

With the shower behind her and permission to take a leave from work, Teresa turned her attention to packing for the trip to Breil. She had left her open suitcase on the bed while she collected toiletries from *le salle de bain*. When she returned with her arms loaded, the kitten she had adopted from Serge and named Jean-Jean had curled up on top of her clothes as though he was packing himself for the trip.

"I haven't even thought about what to do with you," she said picking him up and listening to his soothing purr. She dialed zero to call the front desk. Serge answered.

"What are we going to do with the kittens?" she asked.

"I've already talked to Monsieur la Salle. He said they could stay here, and Mauricette will feed them."

"Jean-Jean too?"

"Jean-Jean too. I still can't believe you named him that."

"Why not with all the Jean-Pauls, Jean-Claudes, Jean-Louises?"

"You have the alarm set for five a.m.?"

"*Oui.*"

"I can't wait for you to see Breil. It's like going

back in time," Serge said. "*Bon soir.*"

"*Je t'adore*," Teresa said breathlessly.

"Me too."

Chapter Ten

In the morning they took a cab to Gare du Nord to catch the TGV to Nice. Teresa had not seen this part of Paris before. The area was more ethnically populated with immigrants from French colonies in Africa. The people looked poorer, and the streets appeared more crowded. Some of the men wore turbans. Muslim women shrouded in black burkas moved together in small groups like flocks of ravens. Pickpockets and beggars roamed the sidewalks. Serge kept Teresa close as they descended the stairs to the bustling train station jostled about by other travelers. Travel posters for Pont du Gard at Arles, the film festival at Cannes, and the casinos in Monte Carlo adorned the walls.

"Have you ever ridden the TGV?" Serge asked.

"No."

"Wonderfully smooth and fast, 275 mph."

"And Nice, is it nice?" she said with a girlish giggle at her silly pun.

"A jewel on the Mediterranean Sea with palms and lovely beaches."

"I do love the beach."

"You'll like the flower market there: bright lilies, fragrant lavender, and roses."

"Sounds lovely."

"We'll buy fresh herbs and vegetables to take up the mountain," Serge said.

When they had taken their seats, he ordered lemonades for them both, and they chatted amiably as the countryside sped by them.

"What are those purple flowers?" she asked when the train slowed.

"Those are lavender fields, the basis of France's perfume business."

"It's beautiful."

"I love the smell of lavender," Serge said. "Especially after a rain."

Later she saw vineyards with grapes beginning to grow.

"They'll be harvested in autumn."

Teresa grew keenly aware of his lean, muscular body in the seat next to her, the warmth of this hip against hers, the stretch of his thigh resting next to hers. His arm dangled leisurely across the back of her seat. Teresa studied his Rodinesque profile, his rugged features seemed chiseled from stone by the master. Yet he seemed unaware of his handsome, animated features.

Serge had not exaggerated Nice. The avenue d'Anglais was lined with tropical palms and colorful hibiscus. From the promenade they looked out on the sandy beach bordering the Bay of Angels. Children, some of them naked, splashed in the waves of the Mediterranean as gulls screeched overhead. Shouts of *"Dites donc!"* echoed from small girls chasing each other in the surf. Bright umbrellas provided patches of blue-gray shade against the white sand. The scent of coconut oil mixed with human perspiration merged into the musky odor of longing. As they strolled along the water line, Teresa often stooped to pick up agates and the occasional rosy hued shell.

She removed her shoes and let the warm, azure waters massage her ankles.

"The ocean is so clear here, not dark and murky like Charleston," she said.

"I've never been to Charleston," Serge replied. "And you have no idea how envious I am of you with your bare feet, and me in this ridiculous cast. If I weren't hindered by it, I'd be swimming now beyond the waves to that sailboat out there."

"It's my fault you can't." She turned to him regretful, sympathetic.

"Four more weeks, and I'll be mended," he said. "No need to look so tragic."

They ate the *table d'hôtel* luncheon at a Tuscan restaurant where two waiters argued in loud Italian until they caught sight of Teresa's pretty figure. Their angry demeanors rapidly changed as they fell over themselves trying to outdo each other in offering her the best service.

Teresa watched a parade of humanity speaking languages that ranged from Russian to German to Arabic sunning themselves, riding bicycles, casually perusing *Les Temps*. She saw flirtatious young couples, overheated parents scolding their errant, boisterous offspring, and sophisticated-looking cinema types. Olive skinned, enigmatic Moroccans and raven haired Algerians, blonde Englishmen, and even the occasional stunning redhead strolled by. The aromas of various foods wafting from the cafes along the shore were equally cosmopolitan in nature.

"I can certainly pick out the English women here," Teresa said with a laugh. "The French women look men in the eye with complete fearlessness. The English look more reserved."

Serge smiled. "I didn't know whether to warn you about the, shall we say, less modest swimwear, but you haven't lost your poise."

"No, I didn't, did I?"

The "Nice Carnival Song" danced from the speakers that rested upon the patio. Serge plucked a yellow blossom from the hibiscus plant in the ceramic planter next to their umbrella covered table and tucked it behind Teresa's ear.

"You look like a Caribbean beauty," he said.

After lunch, they visited the market that overflowed with purple aubergines, shiny green peppers, lush tomatoes, fuzzy peaches, and hearty loaves of French bread. The flower market blazed with color: the exotic bird of paradise, the national flower of South Africa, lavender orchids, and yellow roses. Long stemmed carnations and purple irises, indeed every flower that Teresa could imagine seemed to be represented. She remembered what Serge had said about buying flowers for his grandmother and then learning that she had already passed away. She pictured him tossing the roses one by one onto the heaving waves of the Bay of Angels.

They finished their shopping and took a taxi to the Michelin station, where separate cars on tracks took travelers to the top of the Alps, snow covered now even in summer. This newer form of transportation had replaced the old funiculars which rose and fell based on water pressure. Teresa, dazzled by the whiteness, inhaled the clear, crisp air and enjoyed the azure sky. She concentrated on the scenery and refused to think what might happen if some cable broke, and they tumbled down the steep slope.

At the top of the mountain, they rented a green Fiat and rumbled off in the direction of Breil. The Roya River danced over rocks and boulders beside the road.

Serge opened the car window to listen to the roar of the water.

"I would think you'd be snowed in during the winter," Teresa said.

"Yes," Serge agreed. "But everyone manages. They stock up on necessities and firewood. Some of these buildings are from the 1500s, and the stone walls are more than a foot thick. It keeps the heat inside."

Teresa eagerly took in the medieval turrets and towers, the women with their scarf-covered heads, the men in berets. An ancient fountain in the village square brought water up from an artesian spring, and the villagers still brought their own containers to fill them with the pure, cold water. They passed through the main part of the quaint alpine village, and the Fiat struggled to climb up a tortuously curving road. Evergreens shaded the road. Intermittently, sun peered down on clearings sprinkled with wildflowers. Serge turned left onto a narrow, angular dirt drive and halted in front of a charming home built something like a Swiss chalet.

When she emerged from the car, Teresa inhaled the air pungent with the fragrance of spruce. Suddenly, she was almost knocked down by a huge, extremely friendly Bernese mountain dog.

"Jollie!" Serge called out. "I didn't know if you'd still be around." He tugged the canine's collar. "She's my girl, and I can't have you slobbering all over her."

"At first, I thought he was a bear," Teresa said with

a laugh.

"Jollie is sort of the neighborhood welcoming committee. He's a Berner Sennenhund, a Swiss breed. Some call them Bernese mountain dogs."

"I love his coloring, black and white like a border collie, but the brown patches above his eyes look like inquisitive eyebrows. Goodness, though, he's almost as large as a St. Bernard," Teresa said.

"You'll have to meet his owner, an arthritic old shepherd who still raises goats the old-fashioned way and makes his own butter and cheese. Jollie has quite a personality and is an expert at winning his way into your pantry."

Jollie wagged his tail affectionately as though Serge's complaints were fanciful.

"Let's get unpacked," Serge suggested. "But first, a tour of the house."

He unlocked the front door and led Teresa into a spacious room with a stone fireplace. The room served both as a den and dining area. Wide-planked hardwood floors stretched from one thick wall to the other. Off the dining room stood a roomy kitchen.

"My grandmother was a wonderful cook," Serge said, putting a cloth bag of vegetables on the counter. "She taught me most of what I know. One of her secrets, I believe, was her cast iron cookware."

The bedroom downstairs had its own bath, and the two bedrooms upstairs shared one. The downstairs room had dark paneling and curtains the color of burgundy wine. A masculine sort of room with a heavy walnut desk, brass pendulum clock, and bookcase full of nonfiction and novels. Serge chose to sleep there. It had been his grandparents' bedroom. Upstairs the bedroom on the right had sage green walls and white curtains printed with fern. Rag rugs adorned the wooden floor. The left bedroom was pale blue. All of the beds boasted intricate, colorful quilts Serge's grandmother had hand-sewn, and above each bed hung a brass crucifix.

"In the winter, my grandmother used to quilt," he explained. "There's a basement, but we can see that later. What do you think?"

"Very comfortable," Teresa replied. "And what spectacular views. I need a camera." She looked out of a second story window over snowcapped mountains being painted orange by the setting sun. Serge took her in his arms and kissed her.

"I'm glad you like it because I like you. So which room do you desire?"

"Would I be selfish to say this one so I can watch the sunset?"

"Of course not. I'll have the one right below. Let's open these windows and air the place out." He raised the window allowing fragrant mountain air to enter. "It's good you came with me. Sometimes when I'm here alone, the pleasant memories of my grandparents are too poignant."

"That's one of the reasons I love you so. You're sentimental," Teresa said, caressing him with her smile.

Jollie barked in the yard.

"That's his begging bark," Serge said. "Let's see what we can find for him."

Downstairs in the kitchen, he rummaged in the pantry and dug out a rawhide chew toy.

"This will have to do for the present." He tossed it to the dog who panted just outside the kitchen side door.

"And now to the task of feeding the humans." He brought an iron skillet from the cabinet, turned on the gas stove and poured olive oil into the pan. Soon the aroma of sautéed eggplant, oregano, and sage filled the room. Teresa sliced the bread and slathered it with butter to warm in the oven.

"I don't know if you noticed the stain on the ceiling of the light blue upstairs bedroom," Serge said. "There's a leak in the roof, and I have to replace shingles and repaint."

"But you can't climb a ladder with your leg in a cast. It's way too dangerous," Teresa warned.

"I know," he admitted sheepishly. "Do you think you can help me?"

Teresa smiled. "I think I owe you that and more."

"I can call my old friend, Guy."

"I do know how to hammer a nail," Teresa insisted.

"We're talking clay shingles, so we'll need a trough and mortar. But tomorrow, we'll enjoy ourselves. I want to show you Breil."

\*\*\*\*

Downstairs, Serge walked into his bedroom, the one that had been his grandparents' room when he'd lived with them. The quilt was one he remembered his grandmother sewing in front of the flickering fire. As a boy, he'd sat mesmerized by the movement of the needle and thread diving in and out of the colorful scraps of cloth.

The same furnishings still stood in the same spots. Serge remembered his grandfather resting on the bed, metal moving beneath the skin in his right arm when he flexed it.

"What is it, *Grandpère*?" he asked.

"Come here. You can touch it."

Gingerly, Serge felt the hard metal. It moved.

"It's shrapnel, from the war. The Germans put small scraps of metal in their bombs, and the fiery fall-out embedded itself in the flesh."

"Does it hurt?" Serge asked.

"Not anymore. The doctor said he could remove it, but I told him I'd come back from the war with it and decided to keep it. It would probably hurt just as much coming out as it did going in."

The old man had tousled his hair. Affectionate and demonstrative, his grandfather gave the most wonderful hugs in the world. But Serge would never receive another one of his warm embraces again. He swallowed back a hard lump that had formed in his throat. *What I wouldn't give to follow my grandfather around through the village again to the butcher, the baker, or the fruit and vegetable market. I want to hear his jokes and stories again, hear his laugh, watch him play bowls.*

Maurice Gervais had lived to be eighty-four, but even then it had hurt to say good-bye to the only man who had ever loved him unconditionally.

****

Teresa awoke to the crisp mountain air having slept better than she had since coming to France. The cool air invigorated and renewed her, and she could already smell coffee downstairs. Slipping into jeans and a sweat shirt, she quickly ran a brush through her hair and descended to the kitchen. Serge had let Jollie inside and offered him a thin slice of ham. The dog jumped up when Teresa entered and wagged his tail.

"He's smitten," Serge said. "As I am."

He slid his arm around her waist and kissed her. Their lips lingered playfully, and when Teresa opened her eyes, Serge examined her face with appreciation, his eyes softly aglow.

"The Alps agree with you," he appraised. "Your cheeks are pink. Your eyes are shining like fiery stars."

"I love it here. I can't wait to see more."

"Breakfast first." He pulled out a chair for her at the rustic oak table and put a hot cheesy omelet on her plate.

"You're spoiling me," Teresa said, raising a forkful to her mouth. "This is fantastic."

"I'm just buttering you up for that climb to the roof."

They sipped their coffee, and Teresa arose from her chair.

"You did the cooking, so I'll do the cleaning."

She took the plates to the sink and washed them while Serge put the food away.

He came up behind her and twined his arms around her waist.

"I had difficulty sleeping when I thought of you right there in the room above."

"We made a promise," Teresa said, though she had to admit to herself that her last thoughts before sleep were of him, the smell of him, the leanness of his muscular arms, the softness of the hair at the nape of his neck.

"And I am a man who honors my word," he said. "Let's go for a walk." He was so adept with the metal crutches that Teresa had to speed up to keep pace with him. A frolicking Jollie accompanied them. Just down the road, a stream formed of melted snow rushed over rocks. Serge took her to a waterfall with a deep pool at the bottom.

"As boys, my friends and I would jump from that ledge there." He pointed to a granite outcropping nine or ten feet above them. "I'd go now if I didn't have this cast."

"But it's so high," Teresa observed. "If one of you had landed wrong, he could have broken his neck."

"Boys don't think of things like that. All it took was one foolhardy enough to try it and succeed. Then he could bully the rest of us into trying."

He took a stick and tossed it into the pool for Jollie who jumped in and retrieved it. When the dog returned it, he shook his thick coat spraying them both with chilly water. Teresa laughed, and Serge threw the stick again. As they hiked on through the evergreen forest, they heard tinkling bells. The trees opened into a clearing where goats grazed, and wild flowers flourished. The mountains in the background soared up like the mighty Tetons of Wyoming.

"Why didn't I bring a camera?" Teresa bemoaned.

"There's one at the house. We'll come back at sunset. It will really be pretty then," Serge said. "I'll introduce you to Jollie's owner."

He took a narrow, dirt trail across the meadow to an ancient stone shack with a thatched roof. Smoke wound from the chimney. Serge rapped on the door and a stooped, old man with a hawk nose and wrinkled, leathery skin opened it. His blue eyes sparkled, piercing and intelligent.

"*Bonjour*," Serge said. "Do you recognize me, Monsieur Barbour?"

"*Oui. Bonjour. Entrez-vous.*"

Serge had to stoop to enter, and Teresa found that her eyes had to adjust to the dimness. The tiny cottage smelled musty and smoky. Drying herbs hung upside down from the roof rafters. The floor consisted of hard packed dirt. Descended from sturdy peasant stock, Monsieur Barbour lived much the way his ancestors in the Middle Ages had lived.

"I see you've brought back my wandering shepherd," Monsieur Barbour said, referring to Jollie who had plopped down before the fire.

"I wanted you to meet Teresa Worthington," Serge said. "She's a *bonne amie* from America."

"*Très belle*," replied the older man kissing Teresa on each cheek before offering her a seat by the fireplace. Teresa noted the cheesecloth atop ceramic jars where Monsieur Barbour had been straining goat's milk to make cream and butter.

"Has Serge told you about the *genepi*?" Barbour asked.

"No." Teresa shook her head, mystified.

He gathered some fragile blossoms from his windowsill. "From this little plant you can distill the most flavorful liquor. The mountain goats love it. But it is found in most abundance at l'Arpette, the highest peak. These old legs won't carry me there any longer."

"My friends and I brought many flowers back from our camping trips," Serge explained.

"I remember," the old man said. Then he looked at Teresa. "Go behind the house and bring me one of the jugs cooling in the stream."

As Monsieur Barbour filled his pipe with tobacco and offered Serge a cup of coffee laced with goat's milk, Teresa went around to the back of the cabin.

Lured on by the sound of trickling water, she descended a footpath to the icy waters that served as Monsieur Barbour's refrigerator. Lifting one of the porcelain jugs sealed with a cork, she returned to the cabin.

Monsieur Barbour unstopped the container, poured the golden elixir into a glass, and handed it to Teresa. She looked at Serge whose nod urged her to try it. The smooth, sweet dram tasted delightful.

"Nectar for the gods, is it not?" Monsieur Barbour asked, raising his eyebrows inquisitively.

"I've never tasted anything like it," Teresa admitted.

"The flower is so popular with wild mountain goats that is it very rare indeed,"

Serge said. "On one of our hiking trips, I spotted some on the narrow ledge of a cliff.

"Holding on to a root, I swung my body over to the outcropping of solid rock to pick the blossoms. My friends gasped as my foot slipped, sending a shower of gravel down the two thousand foot precipice. Like a monkey, I regained my balance and rejoined them flowers in hand."

"I remember, I made six or seven liters that summer. You boys and your exploits. Did he tell you that they also found a cave with live mortars from WWII? They're lucky they didn't blow themselves up. But as my mother used to say, God provides special guardian angels for little boys," Monsieur Barbour said.

"I'm learning that he was quite a daredevil. In America, he would have been labeled a troublemaker," Teresa said.

"But he was always good at heart, Serge was."

\*\*\*\*

Alex knew that Serge's apartment had been vacant for more than two weeks.

*He's probably been sleeping at the hotel. What a coward. He'd better not be sleeping with Teresa.*

He took an alley off Garibaldi Boulevard and came up behind Serge's building. Climbing the fire escape to the landing, he broke a pane out of the window next to the back door, then reached in and unlocked it.

The apartment smelled musty. Alex helped himself to a bowl of dry cereal, then wandered from room to room gleaning information about Serge's personal life.

He pulled the knife from his back pocket and slashed curtains, the bed covers, and mattress. He emptied drawers and tossed the contents on the floor. He plopped down on the sofa.

*Sooner or later, he'll show up here. Unless, unless they've gone off together.*

The mere thought made him seethe. He paced the room. He was sick of his filthy clothes, sleeping on park benches, living in squalor. He stripped and turned on the shower letting the hot water build up steam. Then standing beneath the intensive downpour, he let the water scour his skin.

When he emerged, he studied his bearded face, blood shot eyes, and dripping dreadlocks in the mirror. He dried off and took a pair of underwear and a T-shirt from Serge's dresser.

*I'll just camp out here. Won't Frenchie be surprised when he returns?*

Chapter Eleven

"You should see the view from up here," Teresa called down from the top of the ladder.

"Yes, I've seen it before." Serge passed a clay tile shingle up to her along with mortar atop a trowel.

She spread the mortar over the exposed boards of the roof where the broken tiles had been removed and then lodged the clay shingle in place.

"You can see way down into the valley. Tiny roads and tiny cars. A panorama of fields, all different shades of green and gold like one of your grandmother's quilts."

"Yes, I'm sure you can. Make sure that the tiles overlap so there won't be any way for the water to get past."

"I'm putting them in just like the ones above them," she said.

"That's good." Serge looked up at the shapely round seat of her jeans. "The view from down here is rather lovely as well."

"Oh, Serge, you're embarrassing me." She swung around and deliberately dripped mortar on him.

"Nothing to be embarrassed about I assure you," he teased. "When we finish, I want to take you to the village to see the church where I had to do penance one summer."

"Whatever for?"

"I'll tell you the story on the way down." He continued to hand up tiles that Teresa fitted together like puzzle pieces.

At last, they finished, and she descended the ladder.

"You have some mortar in your hair." Serge gently removed it with his fingers.

"So what dastardly sin did you commit as a boy?"

"My grandfather had me go through catechism, and I had participated in my first communion. Then I trained as an altar boy. The church, which I'll show you, must be five to six centuries old. It had a massive wooden door where the small shelves that held the votive candles were stored. I just thought how lovely they would look all burning brightly like a Christmas tree so I lit them—all of them. Before I realized it, the door caught fire. I beat it out with an altar cloth. Ashamed and afraid, I ran off. The priest, of course, didn't know I'd been there that afternoon. It was a great mystery who had set fire to the door. Finally, I told my grandfather what I'd done, and he made me go to confession and tell the priest."

"What did he say?" Teresa asked.

"There was a long moment of silence on the other side of the curtain," Serge said. "I asked what my penance should be, and I was told to come mop floors, clean pews, and polish the brass candlesticks for a month. The priest never scolded or rebuked me in public."

After lunch, they descended the winding road to Breil and visited the church. Enchanted by the stained glass windows and ornate woodwork, Teresa wandered the aisles and examined statues of the Virgin Mary and the infant Jesus. The organist was practicing, and the music resonated off the vaulted ceiling. As Teresa studied the massive crucifix above the altar, she thought of the savior's suffering, his body twisted in agony, his face looked down in sorrow.

Serge talked to the organist in his usual easygoing manner. When they left, he showed her the *boulangerie* and the *boucherie*. They purchased lamb chops for dinner and watched a few older men play a game of *pétanque* on the *boulodrome* beneath the shade trees. Serge explained the rules as the players tried to throw their silver metal ball closest to the *cochonnet*. Between turns, they sipped glasses of pastis, an anise-flavored liquor.

On the ride back in the Fiat as Teresa drove, she told Serge about the minister's sermon at the American Church in Paris.

"He said God is the God of new beginnings and that he's the master artist. It was like he was talking directly to me. As though God had led me to that church on that particular day."

"I'm sure that's true," Serge said. "Just look at that sunset. What artist could create such colors?"

Teresa pulled over to a lookout spot on the side of the mountain. The setting sun turned the glistening snow on the Alps variegated shades of rose and orange. The clouds in the sky matched the snow.

Serge pulled Teresa to him, and this time both their passions ignited, yet he remained tender and gentle.

"This promise is getting very difficult to keep," he said, his low voice husky with emotion. "*Je t'aime.*"

"I love you, too," Teresa said. "Still, we should take things slowly."

"But of course." Reluctantly, he drew back. "I don't want to lose you."

"I don't want to lose you, either," she murmured.

"My grandfather always said don't marry someone you can live with, marry someone you can't live without."

"A wise man, your grandfather."

\*\*\*\*

They arrived at the house just as it began to rain. Thunder rumbled down to the valley. Teresa held the umbrella over Serge as he used his crutches to reach the house. Inside they cooked the lamb chops with onions and spices that made their mouths water and their stomachs growl. Then just as they sat down to eat, the electricity went out. Serge brought candles from the pantry and lit them.

"Just don't burn the door down," Teresa teased.

They let Jollie in out of the storm and then started a fire in the fireplace. After a while, Serge went upstairs to examine the leak in the ceiling where they had repaired the roof.

"Our patch work seems to have done the job," he said when he returned. "That means we can repaint the ceiling to cover the stain. If you don't mind, I'll send you up to the attic tomorrow just to make sure. But right now, let's just cuddle by the fire."

He sat next to her on the sofa and entwined his arms around her. Teresa studied his face in the flickering firelight. His profile was rugged and handsome. Deep dimples creased his cheeks whenever he smiled.

"Have you, I mean, I know you have—"

"Have what?" Serge asked quizzically.

"Been in love before?"

He laughed. "In and out, all the time in secondary school."

"And since then?"

A strained silence hung in the air as Serge struggled inwardly.

"The past is the past," he said.

"No, I want to know. When you first met me, you so accurately appraised that someone had hurt me. I've asked myself how you could have known such a thing. And then it occurred to me perhaps you had some secret sorrow of your own."

"Most of us have secret sorrows as you put it. There was a girl, Janine. I met her when I first moved to Paris five years ago. She lived on a houseboat on the Seine with her parents, an only child. She danced in the ballet. She didn't really come from the upper class like the other dancers, but she was far more talented."

"What happened?"

"I fell quite hard." A pained expression came over Serge's face, an expression difficult to define. *Guilt? Anguish?*

"I wasn't active in the church during that time. I mean I was raised to know right from wrong. But I drifted then. And I'd met this incredible girl. I thought we would marry one day, and Janine, she seemed crazy about me as well. We got intimate too quickly, and she got pregnant. I was so excited. I really wanted that baby." His gaze seemed far away where the pain stabbed anew and cut like a blade.

"Determined to be recognized for her talent and pursue her career, she auditioned for the New York Ballet and was accepted. She didn't want a child. I wanted her to stay in France and get married. When she wouldn't, I begged her to have the baby and told her I would take care of him or her. She told me she'd already gotten an abortion." He swallowed and looked away. "I grieved for my child. Overwhelming guilt brought me back to the church."

"Do you think of her often?" Teresa asked.

"Not since I've met you, and it wasn't really her I thought of as much as the child. I always pictured him as a boy. He'd be four years old by now. I hope this doesn't make you, I mean—please don't think less of me."

Teresa touched his hand, leaned closer, and kissed him.

"I think I love you more," she said.

He kissed her then with building urgency. She found herself matching his passion, swept up in desire. Her body tingled at his touch as his hands roamed over her arms and waist.

"Oh, Serge," she sighed contentedly into his ear.

This time Serge pulled back and studied her face in the firelight.

"I think we better go to bed," he said, "before I break promises I've made to a very important person. Be glad that this cast is such a hindrance." He laughed.

"There's been a movement in England to uphold fathers' rights. Sometimes I think society has gotten everything so mixed up," Teresa said.

Serge studied her thoughtfully and kissed her chastely on the forehead. "Sleep well."

They went to their separate rooms. As Teresa lay down on the bed, she smelled his cologne lingering on her skin.

\*\*\*\*

A shabby vagrant walked down rue Guynemer across from Luxembourg Gardens. Though it was warm, he wore a lightweight, hooded jacket. He pulled the hood up now like a monk in a cowl. He thought about how easy it would be to bury a body beneath the rose bushes except that too many pedestrians strolled about the area, looked at him, and watched him. He stumbled into a middle aged Frenchman on his way to work.

"*Pardonnez-moi*," the older man murmured, but the ill-smelling vagrant pushed past him and darted into a store.

The harried manager glanced up from the counter and watched the shifting eyes of the customer who had rattled the door when he exploded into the store.

"May I help you?"

No reply, only a disdainful sneer and a guttural grunt. The customer walked to the back of the stone shop where hunting and camping equipment lined the shelves. The manager shrugged and returned to his accounts.

\*\*\*\*

Teresa had set the alarm on her travel clock for 6:30 a.m., determined to wake first and fix Serge breakfast. She found the strawberries they had purchased at the market in Nice at the back of the fridge. She rinsed them and cut off the green leafy tops. Then she sprinkled a light coat of frosty sugar over them. Having discovered some blue bowls in the cabinet, she placed the strawberries inside. The color combination was quite lovely. She would serve the berries with milk.

Next, she retrieved some eggs and some slightly stale bread which she cut into thin slices. The eggs she whipped in a bowl and sprinkled with cinnamon. Dipping the bread into the foamy froth, she made French toast. As it fried on the griddle, she brewed coffee.

"Something smells great in here."

She looked up to see Serge filling the doorway, his hair tousled, his white T-shirt stretched across his broad shoulders.

"It's time you learned that I can cook too," she said.

Scratching sounded at the door, and Teresa peered out the window at Jollie. She let him inside and rubbed his ears. He lay at her feet adoringly. After breakfast, Serge wanted to check the leak in the roof from the attic side.

They climbed to the second floor, and Serge pulled the rope that lowered a hinged door in the ceiling. Teresa unfolded the rickety ladder steps and mounted them agilely. She disappeared through the hole at the top.

Stale and dusty air made her cough as she crawled in the direction where the leak was located. The wood remained dry despite the downpour of the previous night. "Looks good," she called down. And then she noticed a worn travel trunk tucked up under the eaves. Scuffed and slightly warped, its brass hinges and locks were rusty.

"There's something up here," she said. "Some sort of old trunk."

"How heavy is it?" Serge called up.

Teresa tugged one of the end handles on the three-by two-foot box.

"Not too heavy."

"Bring it down."

Carefully returning on the boards set over the rafters, Teresa dragged the trunk behind her. At the ladder, she swung her legs over the ledge and holding the rail with one hand, maneuvered the trunk down with the other.

Serge reached up and took it from her.

"My grandfather's," he said. "I must have missed it when I cleaned out the house."

He carried it to the spare bedroom where they would be working. Prying open the latches with a screwdriver, he opened it. Stacks of yellowed envelopes and letters postmarked in the late thirties and early forties stood inside. The envelopes were unsealed, and he opened one, gingerly removing the missive inside. Scanning the cursive writing in the unmistakable penmanship of his grandfather, he let out an awed sigh.

"These are letters that my grandfather wrote my grandmother during WWII when he fought in the French army and later the Resistance."

"What an invaluable gift of history," Teresa exclaimed.

"Reading them I feel like he's right here in the room with me again. I can hear his voice. Some of his misspellings sound like the funny way he often mispronounced certain words. You would really have laughed at his English. It was awful."

"Probably not worse than my French," Teresa said.

"I'll study them tonight," Serge said. "I can't thank you enough for finding them."

"You mean stumbling over them."

"You see, before the war my grandfather had left a successful jewelry business in Paris and moved to Tunisia, a popular French vacationing spot. He sold rings, necklaces, and earrings to the tourists. Many of the pieces were his original designs. He made this ring for me."

Serge held up his right hand. Teresa had noticed the gold circle with Serge's initials before but had not realized its significance or sentimental value.

"When it became apparent that Germany was a threat, he returned to France, but not to Paris. Though he was in his forties, he re-enlisted in the military. My grandmother was fourteen years younger than my grandfather, and my father was a small boy. By the time my father was in his twenties, France was at war again in Vietnam. My grandparents had retired to Breil, and at first my mother lived with them while my father fought in Asia. When he was declared missing in action, she returned to America. By then, I was already Poppy's boy."

"I didn't know my grandparents well," Teresa said. "My mother's parents were English and died before I was born. I only saw my father's parents two or three times when I was small. I envy your closeness to your grandfather."

"I still miss him very much." Momentarily, Serge seemed distant, lost in his own memories. When he returned to the present, he rubbed his hands together.

"So, with everything dry, we can begin to paint the ceiling." He had brought drop cloths up the previous night and covered the bed and most of the floor. Teresa adeptly pried open the lid of a bucket of white interior paint with a flat screwdriver and poured some into the metal roller pan. She attached long handles to the two rollers Serge had retrieved from the back shed. He opened the windows to bring in the fresh air, and the scent of balsam and pine entered the room. The gentle sound of leaves rustling in the wind and occasional bird calls provided background music.

"I'll begin with this side, and you start over there. We'll meet in the middle. Not quite the kind of painting you're used to doing," he noted.

"Much more relaxing actually," Teresa answered. She turned on the radio sitting on the bedside table. The work went quickly. Jollie had been let in at breakfast time and came upstairs to inspect their progress. Outside a squirrel chattered and scrambled down a tree trunk. Jollie barked.

"Sit down," Serge told him. The dog made a circle and then plopped down in the corner thumping his tail on the wooden floor and looking up at them from beneath brown eyebrows.

"The curtains in here need to be laundered," Teresa said removing them from the window to avoid dripping paint on them.

"Renters aren't as good about keeping places up as owners," Serge replied.

He stood back to survey their progress.

"It's amazing how a fresh coat of white paint brightens the whole room."

"I don't know how you manage to balance on one crutch and paint with your other arm, but you're working faster than I am," Teresa said. "Do you have another renter lined up?"

"I'm going to talk to the property manager this afternoon in Breil."

"As I told you, my mother's parents were English," Teresa said. "They lived in London during the war and sent my mother to live with relatives in Richmond, Virginia. Authorities evacuated children from the city. My grandmother died during the Blitz. My grandfather took shelter in the tube station afterward but died trying to help another family escape during an air raid. He practiced medicine."

"Such terrible times," Serge said. "I've heard some Parisians ate rats to survive. Of course, that's why the Brits call us all frogs because they think we'll eat just about anything."

"You should see the Scots," Teresa said. "Have you ever heard of haggis?"

Serge shook his head. "What is it?"

"You don't want to know."

He laughed.

"I do remember one thing about my dad's parents. They brought me a pink clock shaped like a cat. The tail swung like a pendulum, and the eyes moved back and forth as well. Both the hands on the clock, and the eyes glowed in the dark. I hated that thing. At night in the dark, those eyes shining like coals made me hide under the covers. After weeks of little sleep, I finally talked my mother into storing it in the closet."

"I bet you were a cute little girl even if you were a scaredy-cat."

Chapter Twelve

After lunch, Serge took the Fiat down to the village. Teresa stayed behind to take a hot relaxing bath. She washed her hair and scrubbed all the paint from her hands, nails, and arms. She decided to wear a skirt and cardigan and, once her hair had dried, she pulled it back into a chignon. She felt feminine again after all their labor.

When Serge returned, she was curled on the sofa like a cat having fallen asleep reading a novel she'd brought from Paris.

Serge tiptoed from the room and climbed the stairs to retrieve the trunk Teresa had discovered in the attic. He brought it down to his own bedroom and closed the door. He opened the box and removed the letters but was surprised by how heavy the trunk still felt. His grandfather had always been fond of hidden drawers and concealed hiding places, so Serge turned the trunk over and examined the bottom. Rapping each consecutive side with his knuckles, he discovered a cleverly disguised compartment he pulled open. Inside rested a German Luger and box of ammunition. It must have been from a prisoner of war or a dead Nazi soldier.

He lifted the gun and checked it with care. It wasn't loaded. The firearm itself appeared in prime condition. *I'll try target practice with this later.*

Rummaging through the secret drawer again, he discovered a small box containing a ring, a watch, and some gold cuff links engraved with his grandfather's initials.

Then he lay back against the pillows and turned his attention to the letters.

*Dearest Marie,*

*Morale in the trenches is abysmal as you can well imagine. Filthy water gathers after rains, and our feet stay damp. Some of the men have developed trench foot, some type of growth or fungus that itches and reeks. Rations are low, and the food has no taste. I eat only to keep myself alive to come home to you and the boys. The nights are long. We listen to the shrill whistles of incoming mortars wondering where they will land. The lack of sleep makes us zombies during the day.*

He continued to read one missive after another, first arranging them chronologically by the dates in the top corners, until he heard Teresa stirring. Then he carefully hid away the gun in its secret storage compartment and put the letters inside the trunk.

"Good news," he said entering the family room. "A retired couple wants to rent the house for a year to see if they want to move to Breil permanently. The income from the rent will enable me to go ahead with the restaurant."

"We should celebrate," Teresa said.

"That's why I made a reservation at one of Breil's few eateries, La Maison Alpine. You'll like the owners, Jacques and Josephine. I also thought you might want to visit Monte Carlo before we catch the train back to Paris on Saturday," he suggested.

"I hate to think of leaving," Teresa said.

"We still have tomorrow," Serge replied. "We can return in the fall when my cast is off and go hiking."

Teresa readily agreed, but inwardly anxiety already mounted about the return to Paris. *Had Alex left? Had he been arrested? Would he at last leave them alone?*

"What's it like outside," she asked.

"*Il fait beau temps.* It's a perfect evening."

They received exceptional service at the restaurant. Teresa ordered the chicken tarragon, and the sauce was so delicious, she could have eaten it from a bowl as a smooth and creamy soup. Serge ordered the *lapin* and let her try her first bite of rabbit. They finished with chocolate éclairs. Then they strolled next door to a shop where two elderly Belgian women, sisters, tatted lace collars, shawls, and trimmings that they sold to tourists. Teresa watched them fashion their intricate designs.

"This would make a lovely scarf," Teresa said figuring a length of lace.

"Or veil," Serge hinted. He draped it about her head and shoulders.

Teresa blushed, and the two women said something she did not understand. But Serge who apparently did understand winked at them conspiratorially.

Back at the house, they both realized how sore they felt across their shoulders and upper backs from all the overhead painting, so they retired early. Teresa relaxed beneath the quilted comforter and slept dreamlessly.

****

Serge awakened early just as the golden orb of the sun rose above the Alps. He dressed and procured the Luger and ammunition. Outside, Jollie jumped up and followed him, his great plume of a tail wagging back and forth like a flag. Serge strode out across the

157

meadow and lined pine cones along the top of an ancient stone fence.

One by one he took aim and, sighting down the barrel of the gun, fired off rounds that left three pine cones still standing though the majority had scattered on the ground. Jollie whined and then barked at the echoing reverberations. He did not like the loud blasts. Satisfied that the German firearm worked well, Serge returned to the house and restored it to the trunk.

He pulled a small box from beneath the letters, a box he had discovered after Teresa went to bed. He slipped the small package into his pocket.

Teresa came down to breakfast in her pajamas, her hair slightly mussed.

"You look like an adorable little girl," Serge said. "All that's missing is the teddy bear."

After they'd eaten cereal and strawberries, Serge pushed his chair back from the table.

"This is our last full day in the Alps, and I have something special planned." He led Teresa back to the flowing stream. From his pocket he produced a yellowed paper and unfolded it.

"It's one of my grandfather's letters to my grandmother," he explained. "I wanted to read part of it to you:

*Dearest Marie,*

*When life is stripped down to its barest essentials, and every day may be your last, you come to know what is important. How I long to return to you because wherever you are, is home."*

Serge choked back emotion. "I've come to feel that way about you, Teresa. I know you came to France to establish some kind of independence, but I've fallen hopelessly in love with you. I want to marry you."

Teresa felt her eyes fill with tears which Serge misinterpreted.

"Don't feel that you have to answer right away," he said fearfully.

"Yes," she said simply.

"Yes, you want time?"

"No, I want to marry you. More than anything." She leapt into his arms, felt the strength of them encircle her. Their lips sought one another and collided in a spectacular kiss.

"There is something else that I found in the trunk," Serge said. He pulled from his pocket a shiny gold ring with a sizeable russet ruby. "My grandfather gave it to my grandmother, and now I give it to you."

"Wherever we go, we go together. Whatever we do, we do together." Teresa let him slip it onto her finger. Looking at her, Serge finally realized what the expression "stars in her eyes" meant.

Jollie, who happened upon the scene, began to bark uproariously as if he approved. He capered about their feet as if offering his congratulations.

They walked hand and hand up the stream, across the goat pasture where bells tinkled in the crisp mountain air. Serge took her to the terraced olive grove of a local farmer and helped her climb a tree. Then using his good leg, with the crutch as a prop, he came up beside her.

"This is what I used to do as a boy," he said. He plucked one of the ripe olives from a branch and popped it into her mouth. The fruit warm with sunshine tasted salty. They rested with their backs against the smooth trunk and watched the breeze pass through the leaves turning up the silver underside and forming a wave of light gray across the entire grove. Terraces held back by stones climbed the side of the mountain in a series of steps about nine to twelve feet tall.

"I enjoyed growing up here," he said. "They still had the traditional grape harvests then. We would burst the ripe, red grapes with our bare feet in a splashy game. Our legs would be stained up to our knees."

"It would be the perfect place to raise children," Teresa agreed. She tried to picture Serge as a boy of six or eight. In many ways, he was still a boy, full of vitality and enthusiasm, so willing to please and entertain.

"What are you thinking about?"

"What a cute little boy you must have been." She squeezed his hand.

He bent forward and kissed her.

"I'm afraid my thoughts right now are not those of an innocent boy." His fingers lightly caressed her cheek and her lips. "You are all I'll ever want."

****

In Paris, the vagrant stirred beneath the stairwell of the overhead transit. Artificial dreadlocks hung down from his hair, and his cheeks itched with three weeks' growth of beard. He smelled of sweat and cheap wine like the rest of the drunks. Peering through dark glasses, he looked across Garibaldi Boulevard and swore beneath his breath. For days, he had not seen Teresa enter or leave the building. *How had she eluded him?*

Nor had he seen that swaggering Frenchman hobbling around on those ridiculous crutches. When he found the two of them again, he'd squash the Frog, take him out of the picture permanently. Teresa belonged to him. He'd grown tired of her games, of her ploys to make him jealous. He was weary of sleeping on the hard concrete and waking up with a sore neck.

He reached in his pocket and fingered the cold, steel blade of the knife he had purchased at the store that sold camping and hunting equipment. The sharp steel would easily pierce flesh right up to the handle, a good eight inches.

****

The morning of their departure dawned clear and promising. Teresa came down to breakfast to find a gift wrapped package tied with silver ribbon sitting on the table. Serge's eyes glowed.

"Open it," he urged insistently.

Inside lay the lace veil she had admired in the shop. She lifted it gently from the tissue paper and draped it over her head. Along with her waving hair, it cascaded down making a lovely frame for her face.

"It's for our wedding," Serge said simply.

When they had cleaned the kitchen for the last time and inspected the house for any items about to be left behind, they piled into the Fiat and backed out of the drive. The road wound down the hill so steadily that it was difficult not to gain too much momentum. Teresa rode the brake until they reached the flatter streets of the village.

"We'll return the car near the Michelin depot," Serge said, "and rent another at the base of the mountain. Monaco is only about eighteen kilometers from Nice."

"I will miss Breil," Teresa said, "and hope to return soon."

"We will," Serge assured her.

"Then on we go to the Côte d'Azur," she responded with enthusiasm.

Chapter Thirteen

Driving a newly rented, blue-gray Renault, Serge and Teresa stopped at the border of Monaco, the second smallest independent state in the world with the Vatican being first.

"*Cartes d'identité?*" The border control official looked at their passports and Serge's driver's license before motioning them forward. They cruised easily along the middling-high Corniche climbing steadily at first and then snaked down the Maritime Alps to Monte Carlo. The cliffs fell in ledges to the azure waters of the *mer de Méditerranée.*

"I'm glad you're driving," Teresa said as an oncoming car swept by them on the narrow highway. "These roads are treacherous."

"You know, of course, about the tragic death of the American actress, Grace Kelly?" Serge asked. "She died in 1982 in an accident on the *route de la Tourbie.* They think she had a stroke that caused her to veer off the road at a hair pin curve called Devil's Curse."

"She was a beautiful woman," Teresa said. "Alfred Hitchcock called her 'a snow capped volcano full of fire under ice.'"

"I remember when she more or less gave up acting and married Prince Rainier III."

"Was she alone when she had her accident?" Teresa asked, fuzzy on the details.

"No, her daughter Stephanie survived. They fell 120 feet clipping the tops of trees on the way down. Quite a sad ending for a talented woman."

"Yes," Teresa agreed. She looked out the window as the cork oak and twisted dwarf pines shaped by the mistral gave way to tropical palms, lemon and orange trees, and eucalyptus.

The formidable citadel of the Prince's Palace sat upon a craggy rock outcropping. Serge turned off at a lookout where they had a panoramic view of La Condamene, the sparkling harbor of the old city with its enormous yachts and sailboats. He had booked two rooms for two nights at the Hotel de Paris.

"They call the mountain there *Le Chien* because it's shaped like a dog's head," he said as they re-entered the car.

As they wound through the city looking for a café to eat lunch, Serge pointed out the exact city streets that became the racetrack during the Grand Prix.

"So we're actually riding on the track?" Teresa asked in amazement.

"We are," Serge said.

"I can hardly believe it."

"There's the Monte Carlo Casino."

With ornate towers on both sides of the entrance, the casino looked like a palace itself. The copper roof had a green patina, and statues adorned the exterior naves. The landscaping was gorgeous and lush with water flowing down steps to a round pool.

"I don't gamble," Serge said. "I work too hard for my money to throw it away, but we can go inside if you'd like to look around."

Teresa demurred but soon found herself inside the

luxurious casino where she did not feel quite comfortable. They watched a few tosses at the roulette table. Suave men, most speaking French, and glamorous women placed bets.

Shouts of "*Bonne chance*" abounded as the dice were shaken. Fortunes were won or lost in the blink of an eye. The women all wore heavy make-up so that their faces had become masks. In fact, the entire scene reminded her of a masquerade, individuals whose vacant eyes only lit up over a favorable call of the dice.

As though reading her thoughts, Serge said, "They're like addicts. You'd think the idle rich would find better ways to spend their time and money."

The crystal-beaded chandeliers and deep velvet carpets added to the extravagance. Teresa couldn't help but contrast it all with the simplicity of Breil. Even the laughter in the room seemed false, too high pitched and anxious.

"I have tickets to the opera tonight," Serge said. "They're putting on Verdi's *Otello.* I think you'll like it. Are you familiar with the Shakespearean play?"

Teresa laughed. "I saw a musical once in New York, but I've never been to an opera. I read the play in college though, and I liked it."

"It will be in Italian," Serge said, "but you know the story. You'll understand the plot. I like to close my eyes and just listen to the voices soar above the audience."

They discovered a quaint café near the waterfront and ordered bouillabaisse and salad. The saffron seasoned stew of lobster and rockfish and steamy clams tasted delicious and hot. Serge showed Teresa, who was more accustomed to clam chowder, how to remove the meat from the shell. He brought her hand to his lips. "You're my happiness, you know."

At the Monte Carlo Hotel, they obtained their separate keys at the desk.

"I need to rest before our night at the opera," Teresa said.

"Of course," Serge replied, "but it's getting harder and harder to separate from you."

"I feel the same way," she assured him. "We'll marry soon."

They took the lift to the fifth floor where their rooms were side by side. Teresa stood on tiptoe to kiss him good night.

"I've had a wonderful time today," she said. She had not realized how truly tired she felt until she lay down on the comfortable bed. Soon she drifted, drifted. *The car ascended the middling-high Corniche to Monaco from Nice. It accelerated, and Serge, carefree at the wheel, laughed, until the car needed to make a sharp curve. He pressed the brakes, but the car sped up. He swerved to the left. Something told Teresa that Alex had removed the brakes. The tires left the road, and airborne, they toppled off the cliff into space, somersaulting over trees, crashing into rocks.* Teresa started and awakened. Panting, she felt her heart racing. Her body covered in perspiration quivered beneath the damp sheet fighting to regain full consciousness. She dared not sleep again.

Stumbling to the *salle de bain*, she attempted to wash away her anxiety beneath a hot shower. *Why am I panicking? Is it because we're returning to Paris? Are my emotions a premonition of danger?*

She didn't want to spoil the evening Serge had

planned. Turning off the shower, she stepped out and wrapped herself in a thick towel. She draped a smaller one around her damp hair. The only dress she had not worn on the trip was a black one she had brought for church. It accentuated her small waist and rounded hips. She thought about contacting the coiffeuse at the hotel salon to have her hair done but decided against the extra expense. Instead, she styled it herself with a round brush and the hair dryer. Because they had eaten a late lunch, they had decided to wait until after the opera to dine. When Serge rapped at the door, Teresa looked out the peephole and opened the door.

"*Entrez-vous*," she said.

"You are much too formal in your French," he complained. He looked handsome in a black suit, crisp white shirt, and silver tie. His cologne delighted her senses as he gathered her in his arms. "Your chariot awaits, mademoiselle."

La Salle Garnier, a miniature replica of the Paris Opera House, glittered with lights when they arrived. To Teresa, it looked more beautiful than the original in the capitol which rose out of the concrete and asphalt of the streets and sidewalks. The Monte Carlo Opera House had rich green lawns, swaying palms, sparkling fountains, and beds of red, white, and blue flowers.

Inside, the deep red carpets, gilded woodwork, and velvet curtains evoked elegance. Statues and frescos depicted the muses and scenes from famous operas. Their seats were in the center of the rear balcony. Other boxed balconies lined the sides of the opera house. As the overture began, a hush fell over the audience.

The forceful baritone of Othello mingled in harmony with the lilting soprano of Desdemona as they sang of their love for one another. But with Desdemona's departure, the villain, Iago, took the stage. With great cunning, he would convince Othello of Desdemona's unfaithfulness.

Engrossed in the scene where Othello confronts her, Teresa listened to Desdemona pleading her innocence. As though trapped again in the nightmare, Teresa grew strangely agitated as the unbelieving Othello strangled his love. The music rose in chilling tumult.

Teresa thought of Alex's jealous and unfounded rages. When the violent struggle on stage ended, she jumped to her feet and began moving down the aisle.

"*Pardon, pardon,*" she excused herself.

Vaguely aware that Serge followed her, she exited to the lobby.

"Are you all right?" He took her arm.

"Yes, yes. I just feel a bit faint. Let me visit the restroom."

Serge watched with concern as she entered the ladies' room. Inside, Teresa submerged her wrists in the cold water beneath the faucet, then she slipped into a chair and put her head between her knees. In a few minutes, the dizziness subsided.

When it had passed, she rose and joined Serge in the lobby.

"I'm sorry," she apologized.

"You're as white as snow," Serge said. Her hand felt clammy in his.

"I just—the play reminded me of Alex and his rages."

Serge drew her protectively close.

"Do you want to leave?"

"Oh, no! The production is excellent. I'm just being silly."

"When we get back to Paris, we're going to find Alex and confront him. You will see. A quick end is in sight."

Teresa gave him a weak smile, and they returned to their seats. For the rest of the opera, she concentrated on listening to the rise and fall of the voices resonating over the audience. At the end, she and Serge rose in a standing ovation with admiration for the talent of the performers.

Too late for anything heavy, they ordered dessert crêpes at an all-night eatery. "You rest tonight," Serge told her outside her hotel room. "Don't waste another thought on Alex."

Chapter Fourteen

The next morning, Serge thoughtfully got the hotel to fix them a picnic lunch in an oak slat basket, and they headed to Beausoleil. Using a waterproof trashcan liner and duct tape, Serge fashioned a "boot" that protected his cast and allowed him to enter the surf.

Only a few quiet sunbathers and fishermen dotted the sandy shore. By sunset, Serge and Teresa had it all to themselves. Perched on a rough boulder with the salty breeze gently caressing their hair, they watched the sky turn aquamarine, rose, and then pale orange in stages. Gulls screeched above the surf searching for fish.

Neither Serge nor Teresa wanted to leave. They lingered until the moon rose, and they took one last dip in a roofless cavern where phosphorescent colors lit up the sea. The full moon painted a golden path across the glassy ocean.

They clung to each other, undulating gently with the ebb and flow of the waves.

A sea as warm as bath water surrounded them.

"We enjoy *une amitié intime*," Serge said.

"Translation?"

"The most intimate of friendships, but there is also such chemistry between us. Promise that in a few weeks we'll be husband and wife. I don't think I can wait much longer."

"I promise," Teresa said locking her hand in his.

\*\*\*\*

Alex had returned to the platform beneath the train stop and retrieved the bulky backpack he had stowed behind a dumpster.

*Teresa is no better than my useless, damn father. Leaving my mom and me without a word. No explanation. When Teresa's father died, I looked after her. I let her borrow money when she had to pay the rent. If she thinks she can use me and then toss me aside like an old pair of worn out shoes, she'd better think again. I'll teach that egotistical Frenchman what happens when you steal from another man. They'll return soon, and I'm ready. She's going to pay for deceiving me, lying slut.*

In pure anger, he slit open the filthy pillow he had pilfered before moving into Serge's vacated apartment. The feathers inside scattered in the wind and littered the sidewalk. Again and again he rammed the knife into the material, but in his mind, it was body spewing human blood that pooled in a puddle on the pavement.

\*\*\*\*

Though she fell asleep with pleasant thoughts of Serge, she soon returned to the frightening nightmare.

*Serge drove the tortuous roads above Monaco in the inky blackness of night. Then, in that strange way that dreams have of metamorphosing, Serge turned into Alex.*

*Teresa tried to open the car door and hurl herself from the speeding automobile, but the door remained locked and jammed.*

*"What happened to Serge? What did you do to him?" she cried. In a futile attempt, she tried to wrench*

*Alex's hands from the steering wheel. He threw back his head and laughed, a strange, maniacal laugh. With terror, she realized that he was no longer in his right mind. His pupils were dilated, and she saw her terrified expression in their black emptiness.*

Again she woke up drenched in perspiration, tangled in the sheets. When morning arrived, she dreaded the return to Paris. She looked forward to seeing Annette and going back to work, but she felt that Serge was vulnerable. Now that she'd found him, what would she do if she lost him?

Serge displayed none of her concerns. He whistled as he put their luggage in the boot of the Renault. He talked animatedly about his plans for the restaurant as they returned to Nice.

"You know, the American Church has a program with area restaurants where they collect leftover food and donate it to a soup kitchen for the homeless," Teresa said.

"That's a fantastic idea," he replied.

They both dozed in the TGV but awakened disheveled yet refreshed before they arrived in Paris. As they exited the taxi in front of the Garibaldi Hotel, Teresa felt as if someone watched from across the street.

Once inside, they found Monsieur la Salle bent over his desk sorting bills. He looked up as they entered, and the worried expression on his face turned to a smile. Teresa showed him the ruby engagement ring.

"I see congratulations are due." He shook Serge's hand and slapped him on the back. Teresa, he kissed on both cheeks.

"I'm happy for you both. When is the wedding?"

"As soon as we can get it planned," Serge said. "Now that I've found her, I don't want to waste another moment."

"It will be a small, intimate ceremony. Perhaps we could use the courtyard for the reception?" Teresa suggested.

"*Absolument*!"

"Let us put away our luggage, and we'll tell you all about it," Serge said as he assisted Teresa onto the lift.

****

"I've spoken to the minister at the American Church," Teresa told Annette on the phone the next day. "We've decided the wedding will be on July 21st. We don't want to compete with the upcoming Bastille Day celebration on the fourteenth."

"I'm happy for you both," Annette said.

"Are you free this afternoon? I bought Jean-Paul an outfit in Nice, and I want to bring it over."

"He's grown so much," Annette said. "Come over at two o'clock. He's usually awake then. His cheeks have gotten so pudgy and cute."

"You're going to help me shop for a wedding dress?" Teresa asked with excitement.

"But of course."

"And I want you to be the matron of honor."

"Then I better work harder on this baby fat," Annette said with a laugh.

When Teresa returned to the hotel, Serge's shift was ending.

"I need to go over to my apartment to check on things and get some other clothes," he said.

"Okay. Be careful," she said.

\*\*\*\*

On crutches, Serge moved as quickly as most pedestrians. When he reached the apartment building, he took the lift to the third floor where he unlocked the door to C4 and entered.

He halted and stared at the chaotic mess, the shredded curtains, disheveled fold-away bed, broken glass on the floor where the back window near the fire escape had been smashed. The room looked deserted now. The only hiding places were two closets.

Serge took out his cell phone to call the police.

"Put it down," a voice warned.

A wild man with a full beard and crazy, braided hair rose up from behind the sofa. He quickly moved into position blocking Serge's retreat through the door. He slashed at Serge with a wide swipe, nearly grazing his abdomen. "I told you to stay away from Teresa."

Serge lifted a crutch and swung at him. Alex ducked. He crouched down and sprang at Serge with the glittering blade, but Serge deflected it with his forearm. The unexpected move caused Alex to lose his grip, the knife dropped and skittered across the floor. Serge landed a solid fist into Alex's abdomen. Doubled over in pain, he sought to catch his breath while Serge tried to knock him off his feet with a crutch.

Alex turned and fled down the fire escape, the rage of failure consumed him but emboldened his determination.

Left alone, Serge called the police. Officer Gerard arrived within fifteen minutes, and the apartment was dusted for prints.

"You're sure it was Alex?"

"Yes."

Gerard lifted prints from the knife and put it in a sealed plastic bag as evidence.

Serge called Teresa and told her all that had transpired.

"I'll be right over," she said.

She and Annette arrived and cleaned the apartment. Serge nailed a board over the back window on the inside so that Alex could not easily enter again. The police had promised to patrol the area more vigilantly at night.

"It's only a matter of time now before they catch him," Serge said.

\*\*\*\*

To take his mind off Alex and to prepare for life as a married man, Serge lost no time on the restaurant renovations. He hired painters and carpenters who installed the black and white floor tiles within a week. Advertisements ran in the newspaper for a sous chef, prep cooks, and waiters.

While he worked, Teresa finished her murals and resumed her museum work. On Wednesday, she and Annette strolled through shops in the fashion district and tried on wedding gowns and Annette's bridesmaid dress. Teresa showed her friend the veil she planned to use.

They found a gown for Annette at a store named Claire's. The salmon-colored, fitted dress had spaghetti straps and a sheer drape of the same color that rested across her shoulders and flowed to the waist.

"I'd like for you to carry a single, long-stemmed, apricot-colored rose," Teresa said. "You'll look so elegant."

Teresa tried on five dresses, and all of them were

either too frilly, too long, or too maudlin.

The sales assistant studied Teresa's reflection in the three-way mirror. "I think I may have just the right one," she said after listening to Teresa's comments regarding her figure. She left and then returned with a strapless, satin gown. The bodice flared into a white lace skirt that matched very well with the veil from Breil that Teresa had brought with her.

"Oui," Annette enthused. "This is it! Your waist looks so tiny, and your shoulders are beautiful. I have a pearl necklace at home that you can borrow. It will set off your swan-like neck."

"I have a pair of dangling pearl drop earrings that belonged to my mother," Teresa said. She viewed the dress from the sides and, with the help of a hand mirror, from the rear.

"I like it," she said. "But it's a tad too long."

"We can hem it at no extra charge. Just return with the shoes you plan to wear, and we'll pin it up for you."

"Shoes! I'd forgotten all about shoes," Teresa cried with dismay. "I'm not crazy about shopping."

"I know several shops in the area," Annette soothed her. "And I love to shop."

"Okay, okay. We should have eloped in Monte Carlo." Teresa laughed.

She gave the salesgirl a down payment to put the dress on layaway.

"We'll save shoes for another day. I'm too tired to even look," Teresa said.

****

The next day there was still one place near Paris Teresa wanted to visit, and she decided to go alone. She desired to go as an artist seeking inspiration and growth at *les jardins de* Claude Monet in Giverny. With Serge so busy with the restaurant, she booked a minibus tour for Saturday. It would give her time to relax from the hectic shopping and planning for the wedding.

On the morning of the tour, she walked toward her destination full of an anticipation. A black Renault followed her. After she paid seventy-five euros for her ticket, the van driver helped her step up into a blue minibus. In an introspective mood, she moved to the back of the vehicle to sit in solitude with her thoughts as her only companions. She had seen Monet's *Grandes Decorations*, his sixty nine-foot sweeping panoramas of water lilies at the Musée d'Orsay, their light, their color, their reflections the work of a master artist.

A quiet reverence fell over her as she anticipated her journey into Eden.

Monet's home, once a farm called House of the Cider-Press for the surrounding apple and pear orchards, was tucked away in the village of Giverny between Gasny and Vernon. Secluded behind high stone walls, the nineteenth century home of the artist had a barn and studio. The other tourists chatted amiably as the driver parked, and they disembarked.

Teresa had read biographies of Monet, one of the founders of Impressionism, and knew his personal sufferings and disappointments. Many of his earlier works revolved around paintings of his first wife, Camille Doncieux, the love and center of his life. The subject of *Woman with Parasol, Woman in a Garden,* and many other paintings, Camille died of tuberculosis at the age of thirty-five. Monet blamed himself as the birth of their second son greatly weakened her frail constitution. Grief-stricken and bereaved, the mourning husband painted her death portrait.

Left with his sons, Jean and Michel, it was years before he married again, a widow with six children of her own, Alice Hoschede. Alice had helped him raise his sons. Still, Teresa believed his true, life-long love remained Camille.

Crossing from the parking lot, she took in the long, narrow vine-covered house with its green shuttered windows. Brilliant scarlet geraniums made a riotous display of color in the bed along the walkway. The garden had been created for year-round blooms by Monet himself who became an avid botanist. Teresa remembered his comment in his biography: "All my money goes back into my garden...I am in raptures." His artistry lay in double creation, first of the garden itself with planned clumps of flowers and complimentary splashes of color and then their capture on canvas.

Her group toured the house first. The paint in the sitting room, pale blue with deeper cobalt trim, had been chosen by the artist. The ornate cement tile floor harmonized with the Japanese woodblocks with which Monet adorned the walls. A tall, unusual clock painted to match the walls chimed the hour in the corner of the room.

Moving into a small pantry with a checkered rust and cream tile floor, Teresa was charmed by the egg boxes, wooden chests with blue and white painted tile doors depicting chickens.

"Each box held up to 116 eggs," the tour guide explained. "The Monets kept brown laying hens." ,She led them to the smoking room with its maroon and blue oriental rug. Teresa imagined the heavily bearded artist discussing light, composition, and texture with his friends Renoir, Cezanne, Manet, and Pissarro. A bust of the artist by Paul Paulin stood in one corner. On an easel and on the walls, originals of Monet's paintings adorned the room. Teresa drank in the colors. Picture windows gave wide views of the garden.

The guests ascended a curved staircase to the second floor. As customary at the time, Alice and Claude Monet had separate bedrooms with an adjoining bath. Hers was minty green and his ochre with a pale yellow bed. From his second story windows, the patterned expanse of the garden spread out below. Teresa took several photos.

"The dining room is the most dramatic room of the house," said the tour guide leading them down the main staircase into a vibrant, two-toned yellow room.

"Monet despised the heavy, dark furniture of the period and had the china cabinets and chairs painted to match the walls. It was the perfect setting for their blue china."

But Teresa's favorite room was the kitchen. Pale blue patterned tiles throughout and even across the fireplace created a cheerful atmosphere. Cherry brown wood floors and an enormous black coal and wood stove were set off by an array of gleaming copper pots hanging on wall hooks.

Moving outside, they entered the painter's paradise, sculpted nature. Pale pink roses, violet nasturtiums, bright zinnias, and dahlias frolicked before them.

"Monet said, 'I am following nature without being able to grasp her…I perhaps owe having become a painter to flowers.'" The guide finished the house tour.

"You may explore the gardens on your own. Please stay on the paths and don't pick or trample the blooms."

Teresa lingered behind the other tourists. She wanted to be apart, to soak up the atmosphere and ambience of the place. First, she entered the barn that had been Monet's original studio. The loft had a bedroom and bath. How like an artist and considerate family man. In the throes of creativity, he could paint all hours of the day and night, then drop into bed spent and exhausted without disturbing anyone. Next, she visited the studio he had designed and erected later, a building of glass and light, more like a greenhouse. Natural, unfiltered sunlight was the best light for painting. Monet, who specialized in *plein air* often sought the silvery translucence of mists, water reflections, and illuminations.

On the path to the Orangerie where citrus fruits were grown, Teresa saw sagging, green wicker chairs and imagined Monet's second wife Alice and some of the stepdaughters entertaining themselves with needlework in the cool shade of the trees. She felt transported to the 1800s, to a simpler, less hectic lifestyle. Butterflies flittered among the blossoms, and bees hummed as they went about the business of pollination.

Wandering down the center path beneath iron arches dripping with climbing roses, Teresa inhaled the delicate fragrance and touched the velvety petals. Leaving the sunlight momentarily, she took an underground tunnel to the water garden. She managed to escape the crowd and purposely chose the less beaten paths. Above her meadowlarks warbled in melodic unison.

Following the pattern of many Japanese gardens, Monet had dug the pond, enlarging a small brook, the Ru. The arched semi-circle of a green Japanese style bridge appeared ahead of her. Heavy, grape-like clusters of lavender wisteria bloomed in the background. The low hanging weeping willow limbs hung gently like falling tears skimming the water's surface. Water bugs danced across the surface leaving ever widening circles of undulation behind them. Pink blossomed water lilies or as the French called them, *nymphéas Giverny*, floated on flat, round leaves. In an effort to maintain their pristine beauty, Monet had insisted that his gardener row a boat across the pond to clean train soot from the blooms.

Teresa knelt and examined her own reflection in the water. She could almost imagine water nymphs with angelic faces and long streaming hair surfacing from the dark depths of the pond. And then a shadow rose up behind her like a monster emerging from a black lagoon. She thought at first that she was hallucinating. But in a terrifying moment of recognition, she saw Alex, his hair wild, his expression demonic.

Before she could react or cry out, he slammed her forward beneath the water, forcing her head under. She sputtered; bubbles foamed to the surface as she tried to fight back. He was relentless. Pond water entered her nose and mouth. Her burning lungs cried out for air as she choked and gasped. Suddenly, the world went black.

Chapter Fifteen

Water gushed up Teresa's throat and out of her mouth as she coughed. She opened her eyes. An older man arched on his knees above her sat back and allowed her to breath on her own. It took a few minutes for her to realize he'd been administering mouth-to-mouth resuscitation.

"She's all right," he murmured to a cluster of people who had gathered around her. Concern etched their faces.

Damp hair had been pushed back from her face. The front of her blouse was soaked. At least, she had not been found like Ophelia, drowned among the rushes. She tried to sit up but felt dizzy.

"Did you catch him?"

"No. He escaped through the back of the garden, scrambled over the wall. The local police have been alerted. They are conducting a search now. Did you know him?"

"Yes. His name is Alex Sinclair. He's an American. He probably got away in a rented car."

"*Mon dieu!* He tried to murder her," an unknown woman in the crowd exclaimed hysterically.

Teresa's face grew hot with embarrassment. She hated being the center of public speculation, the topic of conjecture. Sensing her discomfort and respecting her privacy, the bus driver of her tour group gathered the travelers and took them to lunch in the village while an administrator of the Monet estate took Teresa to a local doctor.

A gray-haired doctor with an equally gray goatee listened to her heart and lungs and examined her through bespectacled eyes.

"I hear a bit of fluid, but that's not unusual in this situation. I've given you an oral expectorant so that you can continue to cough up the residue."

He also gave her an antibiotic in case she had ingested bacteria from the pond water.

"In a few days, you should visit a doctor in Paris. If you develop a fever, go to an emergency room immediately."

Across the street from the doctor's office, Teresa saw a local retailer and purchased a dry shirt to replace her damp, soiled one. The administrator took her to the police station where she answered questions about Alex and told him about the ongoing investigation underway in Paris. By midafternoon, she rejoined the tour group for the return trip to Paris. On the minivan, she felt like a spectacle again and knew she was the topic of many hushed conversations.

She dreaded telling Serge what had happened, and when she did, his reaction was ballistic.

"You won't go anywhere alone!" he said. "I can't believe no one has been able to find him. I'm sick of police incompetence."

"I'm all right," Teresa said, though it had been the most grueling day of her life.

"*Mon dieu*, what would I have done if I'd lost you?" He pulled her into his protective embrace and held her as if he never wanted to release her.

\*\*\*\*

Cursing under his breath, Alex returned the rental car as soon as he reached Paris in case anyone had noticed the license plate. He had just felt Teresa's body go limp when a noisy gardener had sprinted across the grounds shouting some gibberish in French. He'd been forced to release her and flee on foot. A few more minutes and she would have drowned. Instead news of her attack had been on the radio and would no doubt be included in nightly television news broadcasts.

He had to devise a new plan, a foolproof plan.

*If I can't have Teresa, no one would. With Bastille Day falling on Friday, there will be crowds, confusion, fireworks, and chaos. The Paris police will have their hands full with tourists, drunks, and gypsies. It will be the perfect opportunity to exact revenge. She's humiliated me, played me for the fool after all that I've done for her. All the mutual friends we had who thought our marriage was imminent. What do they think of me now? Spurned. Humiliated. Dumped like yesterday's garbage.*

From a corner gas station, he purchased two one-gallon cans of petrol. A demonic idea had flamed in his over-heated imagination. He concealed the gasoline can beneath a tarp near the air conditioning unit of the transit station. Over the next few days, he planned to purchase a ski mask and a lengthy, fire retardant jacket for himself. The night of his planned arson, he would soak his pants in water to make them less combustible.

Somehow he would turn off the hotel's automatic smoke detection unit that switched on the sprinkler system. He couldn't enter from the rear courtyard because of the loud, pesky canine that had been stationed there since the destruction of the mural. Perhaps he could pose as some sort of repairman. He would give it some more thought, careful, detailed thought. His cunning would surprise them all. He would not be played the fool.

****

"I don't want anything with a high heel," Teresa told the shoe salesman. "And I don't want shoes so fancy that I'll never wear them again."

As he disappeared to the back of the store to search for additional boxes, she turned to Annette. "I don't want to be tripping and stumbling down the aisle."

"You won't," her friend reassured her. At the same time, she examined a pair of black stilettos. "We're hiring a baby sitter for Bastille Day," she continued. "We thought we'd go to the parade with you and Serge and out to dinner before the fireworks at the Eiffel Tower."

"We'd enjoy that," Teresa said. The harried salesman returned with three more boxes of shoes. Teresa folded back the tissue paper and examined each pair before selecting a white pump with a one-inch heel. Sliding it onto her foot, she examined it in a floor mirror.

"These are comfortable," she announced. "And you'll hardly be able to see my shoes beneath the dress. What do you think?" She turned to Annette.

"I think you've already made up your mind so get them already, and we'll go back to have your dress pinned up."

"And then we'll be finished." Teresa sighed with relief.

"Not quite." Annette raised an eyebrow and gave

her a naughty grin. "You still need some lingerie for the wedding night."

"Ooh la la," said the sales clerk.

Teresa flushed a bright red. Annette and the salesman laughed.

"You'll have to come with me," Teresa said when they left the shoe store. "Serge will go crazy if I go alone, but I will not be trying anything on in front of anyone."

They took the *métro* to the Galeries Lafayette near Opera Garnier. Stunned by the Belle Epoque architecture with its glassed dome, Teresa climbed the Art Nouveau staircase in a daze. In the lingerie shop that Annette recommended she looked at silky nightgowns with plunging necklines and selected one that was a dark mauve. Annette bought her two pair of lace bikini panties, one black and one white.

Later, they visited le Bon Marché and Printemps. At the second department store, Teresa selected a gorgeous, translucent peignoir with spaghetti straps that tied at the shoulders. Trying it on in the dressing room, she examined the gentle, round curves of her décolletage. Never had she wanted to give herself to a man the way that she wanted to give herself to Serge. She was glad that she would bring to him her innocence and virginity as a gift. She trembled as she thought about her inexperience and wondered if she would please him.

She remembered her father's advice. "Save yourself for the love of your life, your husband, your life partner."

"What's taking so long?" Annette asked. "Do you like it?"

"Let's just say it looks a lot better than flannel pajamas." She slipped back into her faded jeans and cotton T-shirt and opened the dressing room door.

"Get a whiff of this," Annette said lightly spritzing her with a heavenly smelling gardenia-scented perfume.

"Umm, I'll take it. It's lovely, not overpowering, subtle."

By Wednesday, Monsieur la Salle looked incredibly pleased because the entire hotel was booked as the *la fête nationale* drew close. He had decorated the lobby with banners in *rouge*, *blanc*, and *bleu*. Small flags of the French Republic and the European Union adorned the check-in desk. The *musique* of Edith Piaf and Jacques Brell played over the sound system. It seemed that all of France had flocked into Paris to celebrate the storming of the Bastille in 1789 and the independence of the Republic.

Serge and Teresa were meeting Annette and Guy early so that they could claim a spot along the Champs-Elysées to watch the parade which would travel from the Arc de Triomphe to Place de la Concorde where the French president, his government, and foreign ambassadors would stand.

"*Salut*," Annette called breezily when she spotted them on the sidewalk beneath a shade tree. "Sorry we're late."

"Jean-Paul must have known he was missing something. He took longer than usual to nap," Guy explained.

"Next year we'll bring him with us," Annette said.

They chatted about the upcoming wedding, the latest movies at the cinema, and possible restaurants to try after the parade while other Parisians as well as

187

tourists from around the country gathered along the boulevard. Then the military bands beyond the Arc de Triomphe struck up "La Marseillaise." All around Teresa, French men, women, and children sang out: *Allons enfants de la Patrie, le jour de gloire est arrivé*!

Teresa translated the lyrics in her mind. *Ye sons of France, awake to glory. Hark! Hark! What myriads bid you rise! Your children, wives, and white-haired grandsires behold their tears and hear their cries.*

Cadets from the various military schools, l'École polytechnique, Saint Cyr, and l'École navale marched stridently beneath the arch in full regalia. The blue flag with its circle of twelve five-pointed stars was carried in honor of the European Union. Beside it, the French flag flapped in the breeze. Behind the students, the mounted Republican Guard rode sleek bays who tossed their manes and tails proudly. High-stepping hooves clopped along the boulevard. Medals glittered in the golden sunlight.

Little boys sat on their father's shoulders to see above the crowds. Cheers and applause rose from the throngs. Based on "Ode to Joy," the final movement of Beethoven's *Symphony Number 9*, the European Union anthem wafted above the people.

With perfect synchronization the *gendarmerie maritime* moved past, followed by the Foreign Legion. Then nine jets streaming exhaust fumes of *rouge*, *blanc*, and *bleu* rose from behind the arch and formed a French flag in the sky. Awed gasps escaped the spectators.

As the parade passed, pedestrians strolled into the parks for picnics or disappeared into cafes and *patisseries*. Serge and Teresa followed Guy into a quaint restaurant on a side alley where the waiter seated them and explained the specials of the day. They all decided to have the arugula salad and ratatouille followed by crêpes that had been especially created for the day with red, white, and blue icing.

"Wait until you see the fireworks show tonight behind the Eiffel Tower," Serge told Teresa.

"I'm afraid we're going to have to watch them from the windows," Annette explained. "We haven't been getting much sleep lately. One of us naps while the other does the feeding."

"The problem is that Jean-Paul falls asleep himself after the first two ounces, and he's supposed to have the full four ounce bottle," Guy added.

"We have to keep rubbing his cheek to wake him up."

"Maybe the fireworks will keep him up," Teresa said.

"Let's hope so," said Guy who did have bags under his eyes.

Before returning to the hotel, Serge took them by his restaurant to show the progress that was being made.

"I'm going to install a wall-to-wall mirror at this end of the dining room to create the illusion of more depth."

"Let us know the first night you're open. We want reservations for two," Annette said.

"Now I know where to bring out-of-town clients when I'm on the company expense account," Serge commented.

Teresa felt uncomfortable as they talked. She remembered the prophesy of the gypsy and glanced outside warily. She looked up and down the street but saw only a homeless person looking into a trashcan.

As she and Serge walked back to the Garibaldi, she couldn't shake the feeling that someone watched them. It felt as if a hostile pair of eyes bored a hole in her back.

In charge of the front desk until 8:30 p.m., Serge took his chair behind the lobby counter. Teresa decided to relax in her own room with some soft music and a biography of van Gogh. About 8:20, she came downstairs in hip-hugging black slacks and a silky emerald blouse. Her make-up fresh, she glowed with inner happiness just anticipating her evening with Serge.

Mauricette arrived to replace him, and he and Teresa strolled hand in hand toward the Eiffel Tower. A sprinkling of white hot stars appeared in the clear, ultramarine blue sky. Teresa watched other couples with small children in strollers move briskly down the crowded sidewalk to catch the firework and laser show. She wondered if she and Serge might have a child of their own one day.

Serge hummed "La Marseillaise."

"Look out," Teresa warned, "or I might break into 'God Bless America' or 'God Save the Queen.'"

"Never! Not on Bastille Day, or you face the guillotine."

"How treacherous," she teased.

"Heads will roll," he said with macabre humor.

They found an area across from the tower where they would be able to see above the teeming crowd and waited with anticipation. At nine o'clock, the first bottle rockets shot into the sky and exploded with sparkling color. Lasers danced about the twinkling lights of the tower. Firecrackers exploded like gunshots making Teresa slightly nervous. How easy it would be for someone to shoot a real gun with all the cacophony. *Has Alex purchased a gun?* She remembered his long fingers, his strong hands forcing her head below the water, the terror, the pain in her lungs.

She drew closer to Serge to feel his reassuring strength and warmth. Patriotic music sounded melodiously from the public announcement speakers piped in from a local radio station. Teresa watched the wide, rounded eyes of the children all straining their eyes skyward. Like comets hurling toward space, more rockets burst into a kaleidoscope of greens, blues, yellows, and bright pinks. The foggy mist of gunpowder filled the air with a smoky aroma.

"I've felt like fireworks have been going off ever since I met you," Serge whispered. "Just holding your hand makes my heart beat faster. I adore you."

"I adore you, too," Teresa said. "I never knew I could feel this way about anyone."

When the grand finale filled the sky with and explosion of light and color, Serge bent down and kissed her long and tenderly.

\*\*\*\*

In her room, Teresa relived the excitement of the day and then prayed quietly about her upcoming wedding and marriage. *Keep me safe from Alex. You are my rock and mighty fortress, of whom shall I be afraid?* To continue improving her French, she had purchased a French Bible and begun reading a chapter every night. Tonight, she had started the Gospel of John. Snuggling beneath the cool, muslin sheets, she drifted off to sleep, black, dreamless sleep.

## Chapter Sixteen

Frantic pounding thumped loudly against her hotel door. Teresa sprang to sitting position and listened intently. Something was terribly wrong. Jean-Jean paced the room. The fur on his back stood on end.

"Fire! Fire!" someone behind the door shouted.

As her eyes adjusted to the dark room, acrid smoke filled Teresa's lungs. She grabbed her purse, stumbled to the door, and fumbled with the lock. The door burst open; flames shot up behind a stranger in ski mask. Teresa drew back, but an iron hand closed around her arm and dragged her into the hot corridor. Jean-Jean bolted down the stairs before she could pick him up.

"Drop to your knees and crawl," the stranger commanded in a raspy voice. Coughing and trying to catch her breath, Teresa obeyed. Her heart pounded in her ears. On her hands and knees, it was slightly easier to breath. She descended the cumbersome stairs as quickly as possible.

A wave of panicked guests rolled ahead of her, and one terrified woman stepped on her hand.

Teresa cried out in pain. The hem of her pajama top burned. She slapped at the flames with her free hand extinguishing it but burning her palm.

"*Au feu! Mon dieu!*" shouted a man who beat the flaming sleeve of his left arm with his right. Raucous coughing erupted from people who had inhaled the noxious fumes as they scrambled for their lives. Some noted Teresa and dropped to the floor where slightly more oxygen was available.

"*Vite, vite!*" a mother screamed at her children, then lost her own footing and tumbled headlong down the stairs.

A family of four had taken the elevator to the bottom floor and were trapped inside. The woman pressed her face against the glass as her husband tried to break it with his fist. The children cried hysterically.

"Help them!" Teresa gasped but was jerked in the opposite direction.

Near the front desk, she tried to find her fiancé.

"Serge! Serge!" she croaked. "Where are you?"

The grip on her arm chafed like a manacle dragging her forward toward the side exit. Teresa bolted suddenly toward the room where Serge slept, but screamed in pain as her arm wrenched in its socket.

"Stop!" She kicked at her assailant, suddenly realizing he was Alex. "Let go. I have to go back."

"You're not going back," he snapped and propelled her outside.

Sirens erupted. Two fire engines screeched to the curb, crimson lights revolving and loud alarms blaring. Three firemen descended and connected hoses to the corner hydrant. Inside the cab, another one extended the ladder to the upper stories. An ambulance rocketed to the sidewalk awaiting any injured guests. Police directed people away from the inferno. In the confusion, no one paid attention to two people hidden in the shadows of the exit. The racket of the sirens drowned Teresa's cry for help.

Alex drew a soaked handkerchief from his pocket

and held it over her nose and mouth as she struggled. A faint odor penetrated her nostrils as a wave of dizziness overcame her, and she slumped against Alex who propelled her across the crowded street to the transit station where his car waited.

****

Serge awoke choking on smoke and petrol fumes. He opened the drawer of a bedside table where he had stored his grandfather's Luger and slipped it into the pocket of the cut-off jeans he'd thrown on. He then grabbed his crutches, rushed into the lobby, and pulled the alarm. For some reason he could not fathom, the sprinkler system had not engaged.

He struggled up the stairs against the mob of panicked guests in various degrees of dress and undress. Some wore pajamas; others, like himself, had managed to snatch on a pair of pants and a T-shirt. At the top, he raced to Teresa's room. He threw open the door, but it was empty. Frantic, Serge retraced his steps, his eyes darting through the flames and smoke to catch a glimpse of her.

Back in the lobby, he heard the cries of guests stuck in the elevator, a death-trap. Removing a hatchet from a case mounted on the wall next to a fire extinguisher, he returned to the lift.

"Stand back!" he yelled. "Cover your faces."

With a loud crash, he shattered the glass doors, and the grateful guests tumbled out. Serge urged them through the front door and returned for the fire extinguisher, pulled the pin, depressed the lever, and aimed carbon dioxide foam at the base of the raging flames.

"It's too late," called Monsieur la Salle. He

grabbed Serge by the arm and pulled him outside where firemen shot forceful jets of water from various hoses onto the towering inferno. Serge glanced up at windows where drapes had become walls of fire making a silent plea that no one was trapped inside.

"Is everyone out of the building?" a burly fire fighter questioned Monsieur la Salle.

"My girlfriend is missing," Serge said. "I went up to her room, but she was gone."

"Search the crowd and report any others who are missing," the fireman ordered. Serge looked across the street where many of the evacuees huddled together staring up in horror at the wildly dancing conflagration. The orange reflection of the flames cast an eerie glow about them. One small girl clung to her mother sobbing. She held a smoke-damaged, singed teddy bear in her hand.

"I'll check the guests out front," Monsieur la Salle said. "You look around the corner."

As Serge sped around the corner, he glanced across the street and saw a man slam his trunk door and move around to the driver's side. For a moment, the man looked up. Serge froze as he recognized the face. As fast as the crutches would allow, Serge hobbled across the street. The Renault revved up and bolted from its parking place. Serge memorized the license plate as it sped away.

He whipped out his cell phone and dialed the *poste de police* relating both the street address and the license plate number.

"He's abducted a woman in the trunk of the car and is headed west. Please make this an all-points bulletin," he insisted urgently.

Adrenaline pumped through Serge's system as he paced the street. Then racing back to Monsieur la Salle, he blurted out, "I need your car. Do you have your keys?"

He gave a quick explanation as his boss pulled the car keys from his back pocket.

"I'll drive," the older man said.

As they raced down Garibaldi Boulevard, Serge frantically searched each intersecting street. Numerous dark Renaults cruised the avenues, and his frustration grew. *What if we don't find Teresa in time? Will he kill her? Does he intend to flee the country with her? God, be with her, protect her, keep her safe. Keep her safe for me.*

It became a mantra playing repeatedly in his mind, and he felt a calming Presence that checked his rising hysteria.

Suddenly, they heard the siren of a police car, and Monsieur la Salle took off after it. In spite of the trailing police car, the Renault did not pull over. Instead it sped up, ran an intersection, and made a sharp right turn to avoid capture. To Serge's dismay, in order to slow the fleeing car, a police officer shot from his cruiser aiming for one of the back tires.

"What if he misses and strikes the trunk? Teresa is inside! Bullets could penetrate the body of the car, ricochet and kill her," Serge cried as he braced himself for the sharp turn that Monsieur la Salle made in pursuit. The tires squealed at the hairpin curve. Other drivers honked at them in anger as they had almost caused an accident. Monsieur la Salle ignored them and drove on with steely determination.

\*\*\*\*

Inside the trunk, Teresa stirred to consciousness. In complete darkness, she was jolted to the left and then to the right side of a small, enclosed space. She tried to remember where she was and what had happened. The hazy memory of the fire, suffocating smoke, and then Alex surfaced to consciousness. *Was it a nightmare? Am I still experiencing the nightmare now? Wake up! Wake up!*

A claustrophobic panic grabbed her as she fully comprehended the measure of her confinement. She couldn't sit up. She couldn't straighten her legs. Her body ached all over, and she felt slightly dizzy and nauseated. *Alex must have drugged me.*

Popping sounds like gunfire exploded, and she erroneously remembered the firecrackers celebrating Bastille Day. *Children playing with firecrackers.* The horrifying image of people caught in the glass elevator entered her mind. *Had it been real?*

Her body was tossed up by a bump. She could hear the hum of an engine, the frantic rotation of tires against pavement. She began to feel the area around her, groping in the blackness like a blind person, carpet beneath her, metal above. *I'm in the trunk of a car.* Hysteria seized her. *This is not a dream. I am captured prey.* Remembering the searing pain of her air-starved lungs at the Giverny pond, she wondered what new torments Alex might have in store for her.

*Father, be with me. I don't want to die yet, not when I'm just beginning a life with Serge. I don't want to die.*

It terrified her that any death Alex had in mind for her would not be mercifully short but drawn out and excruciating.

*Give me courage.*

The automobile made a sharp left, then a sharp right. A pain like molten fire shot through her left shoulder.

Teresa reached up with her right hand to feel the spot, and it came away with hot sticky blood clinging to her fingers.

The car crashed suddenly and whipped around one hundred and eighty degrees. A few seconds later, the trunk lid popped up, and Alex jerked her out onto the sidewalk in front of what appeared to be the rear of an abandoned and condemned building.

He hauled her up a short set of steps, kicked open a dilapidated door and shoved her inside. Holding a sharp knife between her shoulder blades, he urged her down a longer set of stairs to a basement. A gray rat scurried out of their way. Teresa heard its muffled footsteps scuttling away and watched its long flesh-colored tail in the gleam of a street lamp coming through a busted window.

Outside she heard police cars arriving. "You're going to be caught."

"I won't go with them alive, and neither will you," Alex threatened.

"Alex, please. Turn yourself in. Please."

They heard the police enter upstairs. Undeterred, Alex slid back a panel in the basement wall that covered a tunnel he had constructed to connect with the extensive Paris drainage system. Pulling a flashlight from his jacket, he illuminated the narrow space and jettisoned Teresa forward before putting the panel back in place. Propelling her with force, they entered a cement pipe beneath the ground. Teresa felt and smelled fetid water as it sloshed over her shoes and ankles eventually rising to her knees. She gagged at the odor.

"Move faster!" Alex snapped.

****

"Stand back!" the police officer commanded aiming his .357 Magnum at Serge.

"No, you don't understand," Serge said raising his arms over his head. "I'm here because the woman who was abducted is my fiancée. I'm Serge Gervais. I made the call to report the incident."

"You're interfering with police business. Move to the other side of the street. Stay there. Or be arrested."

Realizing that precious time was being wasted, Serge and Monsieur la Salle did as they were told.

Two more squad cars tore into the side street. One officer examined the crumpled Renault and quickly ascertained that no one was inside.

Another had gone to the rear of the edifice. "I see where they entered the building," he shouted. The rest of the officers joined him, guns drawn.

Serge watched the windows of the building in utter frustration as flashlights illuminated various rooms that the police traveled through upstairs. His ears strained to catch the sound of gunfire. Inwardly, he prayed as he had never prayed before for Teresa's safety. The search seemed interminable.

"I'm going in," Serge said, but Monsieur la Salle restrained him.

"You heard what they said."

"What's taking so long? They have to be inside."

When the policemen finally returned, they were alone.

"What did you find?" Serge asked coming across the street.

"I asked you to stay back."

"Don't get belligerent with me. I have a right to know."

Monsieur la Salle grabbed Serge's shoulders to stop him from confronting the cop. Officer Ayme, less adamant and more sympathetic than the officer in charge, explained.

"We've searched every room, every closet, the attic, the basement. They've disappeared. Perhaps kicking in the back door was a ruse so we're going to canvas the area on foot. You can do nothing except get yourself into more trouble. Go home, and I'll call as soon as we find out anything."

"Gone? How could they just vanish? There is something you're missing."

Monsieur la Salle moved forward once again to restrain Serge who was rapidly losing control of his temper.

"This is my mobile number." Monsieur la Salle handed his card to Ayme. "Please call immediately. You've no idea of the strain we've been under tonight."

La Salle compelled Serge back toward the car. In frustration, Serge slammed his crutch against a tree trunk.

"They are somewhere in that house! I'm not leaving."

"Get in the car," Monsieur la Salle urged in a low voice.

Inside the auto, Serge punched the dashboard. Pent-up emotion boiled inside him.

Monsieur la Salle had never seen him so

overwrought.

"Let them spread out through the area, and I'll keep watch while you go search the house yourself," la Salle advised. "But you need a weapon of some sort."

"I have one," Serge responded by removing the Luger from his jeans. "It was my grandfather's. I brought it back from Breil just in case something happened."

Monsieur la Salle's eyes had grown wide, and his eyebrows rose.

"Do you know how to use it?" he asked, his voice incredulous.

"I've practiced at a shooting range."

"If I see the police returning, I'll flash the headlights, so keep looking out of the windows."

## Chapter Seventeen

The gruesome conduit beneath Paris narrowed.

"Crawl!" Alex ordered, shoving her down gruffly.

Teresa dropped to her hands and knees. Her cotton pajamas reeked of smoke and now sopped up the disgusting, muddy water. Discarded cigarette butts and other litter floated past them. She could barely see ahead in the dim light of Alex's flashlight. Her neck and back ached.

"Where are we going?" she asked.

"Just keep moving."

"Do you know?" she demanded.

"Don't test my patience."

The water was rising, and Teresa felt nauseated. She gagged but did not retch. "I feel sick."

"Move! We're almost there."

Then Teresa saw ahead to a gaping hole in the right side of the cement pipe. Obviously man-made, she wondered momentarily if Alex had used a pickaxe to create the aperture. The lower part of the hole was higher than the level of the rancid water.

"In there," Alex ordered.

She stared into the blackness. "What is it?"

Alex illuminated the crypt with his light, and Teresa tried to interpret what she saw: uneven walls, a doorway surrounded by orbs, a floor littered with dried reeds. No, they weren't reeds; they were bones. And the orbs were skulls! The catacombs! Her heart pounded in her chest like a jackhammer. Alex had withdrawn his knife. The blade glittered in the dim light of the torch which cast luminous shadows on the walls. *What better place to kill someone? What was another set of bones among the many? Lord, as you helped the Christians long ago who met secretly in catacombs, help me.*

\*\*\*\*

Serge took a flashlight from the glove compartment and crossed the street. More than ever he cursed the awkwardness of the crutches that made movement cumbersome. Once inside the abandoned building, he checked each room methodically, painstakingly. He ripped open every cabinet and closet. He even shined the light up the several chimneys. Last, he descended the basement steps.

In spite of the low hanging cobwebs and scampering cockroaches, Serge tapped the walls keenly listening for a hollow sound. At the panel behind which Alex and Teresa had disappeared, he paused and rapped his knuckles against the wood. Leaning down, he examined the edges and removed the panel revealing the water conduit.

*This is how they vanished.* Moving back up the staircase with speed and dexterity, he glanced out a window and saw Monsieur la Salle flashing his headlights. Serge didn't care. He exited the house and purposefully accosted Officer Ayme.

"I thought I made it clear—" the officer began, but Serge interrupted.

"I found out how they disappeared. Check the basement. You'll see for yourself. I can't spare a moment of time." Serge strode across the street, digging in the crutches with determination at each step. He panted from exertion and dripped perspiration.

"We need a map of the city's underground drainage system," he told Monsieur la Salle as he slid into the passenger side of the car. "They escaped through an underground conduit."

"Where?"

"The left side of the building heading southwest."

Monsieur la Salle contemplated Serge's description and then said that the pipe probably emptied into the Seine. He turned the car in that direction.

"Maybe he plans to escape by boat."

"Hurry!" Serge urged.

When they reached the river, they parked and decided to split up in two directions. Serge went left and Monsieur la Salle went right. The riverbanks were empty except for a few bars where patrons drank wine and flirted with women. A silver moon shone in the sky and reflected off the water. Serge lifted another prayer for Teresa's safety.

He walked the sidewalk close to the river's edge searching for a bubbling flow of water that might indicate current from a conduit. When he sighted such a phenomenon, he knelt and examined the structure. He could see that the pipe was sealed with an iron casement resembling a hard metal net. It was securely bolted in place, and he could conceive of no way that someone could have broken through the obstruction. He pulled his cell phone from his pocket and conferred with Monsieur la Salle.

"I've discovered the same type of construction on this end," said the older man.

"There must be some other way," Serge said in

exasperation.

"I've been thinking that perhaps..." Monsieur la Salle paused.

"Yes, what is it?"

"They've gone underground literally, yes? What about the catacombs?"

Serge had heard of the crypts beneath the city that held the dead, but he had never ventured into them. But Monsieur la Salle, who had lived in Paris all of his life, knew of several entrances where tour guides took tourists into the macabre vaults of the dead.

****

Teresa looked at the vacant eye sockets and mocking grimaces of the skulls surrounding the doorway. They seemed to be laughing at her. Stale, suffocating air seared her lungs. The crimson stain just below her shoulder widened with fresh blood. She dropped to the floor as though in a swoon, but she was conscious. Instead, her hand closed around a femur, the longest bone in the human body.

She jumped up and whirled about slamming the bone into the side of Alex's head with a thud. Howling in pain, he raised his hand to his cheek, and Teresa bolted through the passageway of skulls into the corridor of carnage. Alex recovered and charged after her ready for revenge.

She had a slight head start and sprinted like a frightened doe startled from a thicket. As she continued her headlong flight, the darkness engulfed her. She had to slow down and grope her way along the wall. Her heart pounded in her chest, and the thought occurred to her that she might be heading toward a dead end. The idea fed her rising hysteria. *Dead end? Of course, it will be a dead end one way or another. I'm losing my mind.* Her arms and legs trembled.

The corridor came to an abrupt stop with one tunnel leading to the left and another to the right. She chose the left and found that it made a curve. She rounded the curve and found herself in a nave up against a wall of bones. *Don't scream,* she told herself. She started to retrace her steps but heard Alex. He would reach the crossed paths as well. Noiselessly, she retreated to the crypt and waited, every muscle tense, her ears alert to the slightest sound. *Oh Lord, please let him turn right.*

The beam of his flashlight search the left end of the tunnel. Then it disappeared. She hardly dared to breathe. *He must be surveying the right tunnel. He's trying to decide which passageway to take. If he takes the right tunnel, I'll retrace my steps and go back to the water conduit. But if he comes this way...* She didn't want to finish her thought. Her fingers gripped the femur still in her right hand. *I'll use it like a baseball bat.*

****

Monsieur la Salle parked near the Paris Opera House and led Serge to a narrow alley. "There is a catacomb tour," he said. "The guide begins his presentation here." He showed Serge the entrance to the world of the dead. A bolted and locked door blocked their entrance.

"Now what?" Serge demanded, angry and frustrated. "Teresa may be dead."

"Let cool heads prevail," Monsieur le Salle counseled. He took out his ring of keys to which was attached a miniature jack knife with several different blades including a screwdriver. "I take this wherever I go."

Using the screwdriver, he loosened the screws that held the latch to the door. It gave way, and the portal revealed itself.

"*Voilà!*" la Salle announced obviously quite pleased with himself. "*Après vous.*"

Serge had the flashlight from the car and illuminated the tunnel. The ghastly smell of death and decay revolted him. Giving the light to la Salle, he steadied the gun in his right hand. He felt like Hermes trying to retrieve Persephone from Hades. Passing through a threshold of skulls, Serge had absolutely no idea which way to turn in the grim labyrinth. He moved by instinct and became agitated each time they had to choose a direction. Monsieur la Salle, who had a vague mental map of the city's construct, advised Serge from time to time.

"We don't even know that they are here at all," Serge complained. "This may be a futile goose chase."

"Don't despair," the older man counseled.

"This place is like hell," Serge said. "How will we ever find our way out again?"

"I'm composing a pattern in my mind of right and left turns. We'll just go the opposite directions on the way out."

"*Arrête!* Listen," Serge whispered. Both men stood perfectly still. In the tomb-like silence, they thought they heard the reverberation of footsteps. Or were their fevered minds imagining the sound the way a person alone in a house at night often hears curious or threatening creaks and groans?

\*\*\*\*

207

Teresa left her crypt cautiously proceeding back to the intersection of the dark damp corridors. She heard the receding footfalls of Alex's flight down the right tunnel. She bolted down the passageway to the cavern where she had first fought with him. Her only means of defense, the femur of some long dead Frenchman, she gripped so tightly her fingers felt numb.

With terror, she realized that Alex's footsteps now increased in volume. Aware that he'd been duped, Alex had whirled around muttering curses and expletives of the foulest nature. Teresa sprinted toward the water conduit, but in her panic, she slipped on the bone scattered floor and lay sprawled and helpless.

Attracted by the noise, Alex knew he did not need to search the left tunnel. His quarry had doubled back like some crafty fox at bay. Teresa leapt to her feet ignoring the painful abrasion in her right knee. She was too late. Alex threw himself at her like a fullback tackling an opponent in American football.

Teresa screamed at the pain of his full weight bringing her down. She managed to swing her weapon at him, but the ancient bone cracked in two. Alex rolled off her, grabbed her by the neck, and flung her to the wall.

"How dare you treat me like dirt," he snarled. His mouth violently assaulted hers. His teeth drew blood from her soft lips. His hands groped her as his body pressed against her, cementing her to the cold wall.

"Stop it!' she stammered.

"You want to save yourself for your husband." Alex laughed hysterically.

Teresa scratched his face like a cat caught in a corner, but his left hand closed around her throat, cutting off oxygen. She felt dizzy, limp, and then slumped into oblivion.

****

Certain that they'd heard footfalls ahead, Serge and Monsieur la Salle sped forward. As they rounded the bend, they entered the chamber where Alex stood flashlight in hand hovering over Teresa's slumped body. A raised silver blade was raised ready to plunge into her chest.

"NO-O-O!" Serge shouted. He aimed the pistol at Alex and fired. The sound of the shot ricocheted and echoed throughout the labyrinth. Alex dropped with a resounding thud, and Serge raced to Teresa. Her motionless, pale form appeared a cold corpse. Tears streamed down his cheeks. He raised one hand in despair massaging his forehead.

Monsieur la Salle put his ear to her chest. Her heart still beat. He listened to her ragged, shallow breathing.

"*Elle n'est pas morte,*" he cried jubilantly. Serge crouched next to him on the floor, gathered Teresa in his arms, and felt the warmth of her body.

"Serge," she murmured. Her eyelids quivered, then opened.

From the water conduit, they heard muffled voices, and then the head and arms of Officer Ayme emerged. He crawled into the chamber followed by another police officer. Like Serge and Monsieur la Salle, their uniforms were soiled, their hair festooned with dust and cobwebs.

"*Mon dieu!*" Ayme exclaimed, then stooped to examine Alex's body checking for a pulse that no longer existed. "And the *mademoiselle*?"

"I've been shot," Teresa replied in a raspy voice.

"It hurts to talk."

"Don't try to talk." Serge comforted her. He directed his flashlight at her.

"Your neck is bruised. There's blood on your shoulder. We need to get her to a hospital," Serge said. He stood lifting her in his arms. Her legs dangled toward the bone-strewn floor. Serge turned so that she was shielded from the grotesque view of Alex's sprawled body.

"Shot?" The officer had seen only an evil curving blade on the ground beside Alex.

"Yes," Serge said with anger and impatience. "One of your own guns wounded her when you shot at the car trying to blow out the tires."

Ayme checked his own rising temper and stifled a comeback. He certainly didn't want the department to accused of incompetence or worse.

"Yes, we will get her to the hospital immediately. And then you will all have to give me your statements."

"I think I can walk," Teresa said though her legs wobbled and trembled when Serge set her down. She leaned heavily against him for support as they wound back though the macabre burial labyrinth. Monsieur la Salle and the other officer bore the heavy, limp body of Alex Sinclair, the front of his shirt a damp, mahogany stain.

Calling ahead on his portable radio, Ayme summoned an ambulance and police escort to await them.

When they emerged from the halls of death, the red lights of emergency vehicle and the flashes of police cruisers pulsated like strobe lights. Sirens blared for a second time that night. EMTs secured Teresa to a cot and whisked her off to All Saints Hospital, and the corpse of Alex Sinclair was transported to the morgue for investigation.

"No doubt you shot the deceased?" Ayme asked Serge.

"Oui." He showed the police officer the Luger.

"My word." The law enforcement official handled the firearm with admiration, turning it over in wonder.

"My grandfather brought it back from the war."

"He had to shoot him," Monsieur la Salle insisted. "At the time, Sinclair was about to stab Miss Worthington."

"I see. You will both be available for questioning later?" said Ayme. The phrase was more statement than question.

Both men nodded.

"Then I trust you will want to go to the hospital at this time?"

Relief filled Serge's face. He'd been antsy to follow the ambulance and eager to make sure that Teresa was indeed all right.

"*Merci, merci.*"

He and la Salle hurried to the car and drove to All Saints where they had Teresa's physician paged.

"Her wound is clean," said Dr. Corvetti, an Italian who had immigrated to France. "The bullet entered just below the shoulder here." He touched his own torso to demonstrate. "And it exited in the back. She'll be bruised and sore, but there should be no permanent damage."

"Can we see her?" Serge's voice was anxious and full of concern.

"She's mildly sedated to keep her comfortable, but

yes, you can visit briefly in room 225."

"I'll let the two of you have your privacy," Monsieur la Salle said, settling into a gray metal chair in the waiting room.

Serge left in search of room 225, his shoes squeaking on the sanitized, industrial strength gray linoleum. The sterile smell of bleach and antiseptic filled his nostrils. How he hated hospitals.

When he located the room, he entered softly. Teresa's eyes were shut, and she looked vulnerable, innocent, and child-like. A wrapped bandage engulfed her chest and shoulder, and her filthy pajamas had been replaced by a nondescript, baggy hospital gown. Her honey colored hair appeared matted and dirty.

*My little bird has a broken wing.* He bent down and kissed her forehead.

"Serge?" she questioned opening her eyes. She inhaled his reassuring scent, his strength, his love.

"I'm here," he said.

"What happened? I've been trying to remember everything, but I can't. I blacked out, and then there was a loud noise."

"Alex can't bother you anymore." Fire leapt in Serge's eyes.

"He's been arrested?" Teresa asked, her own eyes round and questioning.

"He's dead." Serge's voice was a whisper. He supposed later that he might feel some qualms, even guilt for having killed a man. Perhaps he could have taken Alex alive, but his reactions had been instantaneous, his only thought, Teresa's safety.

Would she think less of him for killing a man? Her forehead wrinkled in bewilderment as she tried to summon up images from memory.

"He tried to kill me," she rasped, speech obviously painful.

"We don't have to worry anymore," Serge said soothingly.

"The police shot him?" she mumbled, closing her eyes.

"Quiet now. Don't worry yourself." He gently brushed her hair back from her forehead and let her sleep. *Perhaps she's worried I'll be arrested.*

An efficient nurse, carrying Teresa's medical chart, entered the room and told him visiting time was over. He nodded.

"Take good care of her," he said. "She is my life."

"We will. She'll probably be released in a few days as long as infection doesn't set in." The nurse gave him a reassuring smile.

He returned to the waiting area where he found Officer Ayme questioning Monsieur la Salle. Serge heard the officer say, "Of course, I'll need to question Monsieur Gervais, but it appears he is to be commended for his assistance in apprehending a criminal."

"Thank you," Serge said, as he joined the two men.

"How is Miss Worthington? She is well, *oui*?" Ayme asked.

"Yes. And what of Alex Sinclair?" Serge asked.

"He falsified a driver's license and rented a Renault under the name of Roger Whitlock. The manager of the rental car company remembered his face. I assume that Sinclair meant to kill you when he ran you down on your bicycle near the hotel. He has apparently been hiding by impersonating a homeless

213

person, sleeping in the transit stations and parks. While the investigation is not closed, he is a chief suspect in the arson of the Garibaldi Hotel. Somehow he must have dismantled the automatic sprinkler system. It did not come on after the fire started. Fortunately, there were no fatalities and only a few serious injuries."

"I'm glad my insurance premiums are paid up," said Monsieur la Salle. "Still, it will take a long time to rebuild and reopen. Teresa told me of your plans for the restaurant, Serge. I may need to work for you during the interim."

"I would like nothing better," Serge answered.

"I started my career as a waiter, but I hope I will not end it as a waiter." He laughed.

"We will look forward to new beginnings," Serge replied suddenly aware of his exhaustion. The adrenaline rush that had boosted him since the start of the fire had abruptly ended.

"I feel like I've been run over by an eighteen-wheeler," he said.

"You look like it too. Come on and spend the night with me and Marie. You know she'll fuss over us both."

## Chapter Eighteen

Monsieur la Salle, Teresa, and Serge sifted through the charred remains of the Garibaldi, a shell of its former structure. The scorched cinder block exterior walls remained intact, but the four stories of inside walls and floors had been consumed by the raging fire. The smashed elevator stood jammed on the first floor because the steel elevator shaft had not burned.

"At least, someone rescued all the kittens, and Mimicry," Teresa said.

"And no one was killed," added la Salle.

"Still, it must be especially difficult for you." Serge addressed his boss. "To see everything you've worked for all these years literally go up in smoke."

"If this had happened when I was young, it would have been a tragedy to me, but over the long years, I've learned that material things can be replaced. The important things are people, family, and relationships. *Mieux vaut tard que jamais.* Better to learn late than never, right? Besides, I've met with the insurance adjuster, and I should be able to rebuild. I have some savings of my own to add a few improvements and update the décor. We must be positive. Who knows? Perhaps the changes will draw more patrons."

Teresa looked at the courtyard where she had hoped to hold her wedding reception, now a hopeless mess. Marred by ash and soot, the mural contained sections where paint peeled from the intense heat of the fire.

"So much for our outdoor reception here," she lamented.

She had talked to Reverend Salley at the American Church, and he had agreed to perform the wedding ceremony in the sanctuary on July 21$^{st}$ as they had planned. "We can have the reception in the restaurant," Serge said, wrapping his arm around her waist in empathy. "It can coincide with the grand opening weekend. My staff can prepare the food. We have only a small party, Monsieur la Salle and his wife, my great aunt from Lyon, Guy and Annette, Mauricette, and a few of your friends from the museum staff and a few of my friends. Fifty to sixty guests. Unless of course, there are relatives in America you'd like to invite."

"No," Teresa said. "You're all the family I have."

"Then adopt me as an uncle," Monsieur la Salle said, "or a jolly *grandpère*. Whenever you feel put out with my nephew here, you come to me." He patted Serge's shoulder.

"You have been so welcoming to me from the very beginning. I want you to know how much I appreciate you," Teresa said.

Feeling sentimental, the older man kissed her on each cheek. Then looking around one last time, he said, "I think there is nothing here to salvage."

The next morning, Teresa accompanied Serge to the doctor to have his cast removed. The skin beneath it looked pale and clammy. Serge complained that it itched.

"You have no idea how good it feels to get rid of that encumbrance," Serge said. "I feel like an uncaged bird. Now I can finally take my fiancée dancing." He stood up and swirled Teresa in an underarm turn.

"Your x-ray looked good. The bone has knitted together nicely," the doctor assured him. "Feel free to trip the light fantastic, as they say."

That evening they danced along the Seine holding onto each other in the silvery moonlight. Teresa had no idea that Serge was such a good lead. They waltzed and tangoed moving in synchrony to the pulse of the music. Other patrons of the café stopped and watched them as though they were professionals. Serge lunged and dipped her with dramatic flair, and spontaneous applause erupted. Teresa blushed, but Serge took it all in stride. He knew some of the fast, rhythmic Latin dances, salsa, samba, and cha-cha. Teresa found herself being whirled about in quick turns until her cheeks flushed, and she panted to catch her breath.

"You told me that you liked to dance," she said, "but I had no idea how good you were. I can barely keep up."

"It's good that we'll have lots of years to practice together."

"We must definitely have music at the reception," she said. "I don't know when I have ever had such fun."

They sat down at a table so that Teresa could rest.

"You see, I am a man of surprises, a man of mystery," Serge teased. "I'm not hurting your shoulder, am I?"

"No, besides, I'm so high on endorphins, I doubt I can feel pain. I love you so."

"*Serez-vous être ma femme?*" he asked.

"Yes. *Serez-vous être mon mari?*"

"*Absolument!*"

After a few minutes of watching other couples dance, they strolled back to Guy and Annette's flat where Teresa was staying until the wedding.

"You're very quiet," Serge observed. "What are you thinking?"

"That it's nice to be able to walk down the street and not feel all the time that someone is watching and waiting. You're quiet too. What were you thinking?"

"That this time next week we'll be husband and wife," Serge said. "You don't mind, do you, if we put the honeymoon off until fall. I don't feel this is the right time to be away from the restaurant with it just opening."

"Of course, I don't mind. Just you and me in your flat with our kittens that is all the honeymoon I want."

They kissed with great anticipation of the coming week right on the public sidewalk. Pedestrians smiled at the happy couple.

"I want everyone to know how much I love you," Serge said.

****

When Teresa went to pick up her gown with Annette and Jean-Paul in tow, she tried it on one last time. The length was perfect, but the scar from the bullet wound was quite visible on her shoulder. Annette saw her friend's concern and came to the rescue.

"We'll put a lace strap from here to the back and pin a white orchid corsage in place. No one will see the scar," her friend assured her.

"It's just that I want to look perfect for Serge on that day," Teresa said. "I don't want any reminders of all the horror we've been through."

"But of course. What bride does not want to be

perfect on her wedding day?"

Next, they went to a jeweler where Teresa had ordered Serge's gold band. Inside she had the engraver inscribe her sentiments with the single word "Forever." Her eyes misted, and she squeezed her friend's hand. "I love him so much it hurts."

Annette laughed. "You're more emotional than I was when I was pregnant, and that's saying a lot."

They picked up Annette's dress and bought a pair of bone colored pumps for her, sensible shoes that could be worn on many other occasions.

"That's everything then," Teresa said.

"I hope it won't be long before you have your own little Jean-Paul."

"I hope so too."

\*\*\*\*

The evening of the wedding was clear and fortuitous. In the changing room of the church, Serge studied himself in the mirror. The black tux and crisp white shirt with French cuffs fit him perfectly. His usually unruly hair had been tamed into place.

"Don't worry," Monsieur la Salle told him. "You look dashing and debonair, and everyone is going to have their eyes on the bride, not you."

Serge grinned. "So true. So very true."

Then pacing agitatedly around the room, he began to fret. "Do you think she's here? Do you think she's ready?"

"I have it on the best authority that she is getting dressed right now. You won't have a run-away bride on your hands. Now I must go await her in the vestibule. Do calm down. You're working yourself into a frenzy. Sit and take some deep breaths." With that advice the older man left.

Outside the door, Serge could hear the violinist playing the prelude. Cracking the door, he saw the white roses backed by palm fronds decorating the altar. Two candelabras of flickering white candles stood on either side. The minister, Richard Salley, in his white robe stood before the altar in front of the guests. The end of the prelude was Serge's signal to enter and walk to the side of the clergyman which he did strolling as though he were in a dream.

Then Mendelssohn's "Wedding March" sounded, and he saw Teresa at the back of the church coming down the center aisle on Monsieur la Salle's arm. Serge had never seen a woman more radiant. When she reached him, he took her tremulous hand and wrapped it confidently in his own. *This woman, this beautiful woman, is going to be my wife.* Tous mes jours et mes nuits, je donne à toi, à toi seule. *All my days and all my nights I give to you and you alone.*

Reverend Salley looked at them both earnestly before addressing the congregation.

"Marriage is an honorable estate, not to be taken lightly. It symbolizes the mystical union of Christ with his holy bride the church. As Christ laid down his life for the church, so a man should cherish and esteem his wife. As the church waits for Christ's return with whole-hearted devotion, so the bride should cherish and esteem her husband. These two people standing before you promise to love and honor one another in sickness and in health, in time of prosperity and in time of need."

"Do you, Serge Gervais, take this woman to be your lawfully wedded wife and forsaking all others keep thee only unto her as long as you both shall live?"

Looking into Teresa's innocent, upturned eyes, Serge answered without hesitation. "I do."

"And do you, Teresa, take Serge to be your lawfully wedded husband and forsaking all others keep thee only unto him as long as you both shall live?"

"I do." She smiled at Serge with full trust.

"As a circle is eternal so the wedding band symbolizes eternal love," said the minister as Serge removed a gold band from his pocket and repeated after the clergyman.

"With this ring, I thee marry. Let it be a token of our undying love and devotion." He slid the ring gently onto her finger.

Teresa held his ring in her right hand and repeated, "With this ring, I thee marry. Let it be a token of our undying love and devotion." She too slid the ring onto his finger.

"In the scriptures it is written that two shall become as one, and this couple has chosen to represent this oneness through the lighting of the unity candle."

Serge and Teresa each stepped forward and removed a flickering candle from one of the gold candelabras. Then stepping up to the altar, they joined their two fragile lights to a single candle, a steadier, stronger blaze. Teresa blew out her single candle. Serge extinguished his. *No longer two solitary people searching and alone, but one soul beating with two hearts.*

"What God has joined let not man put asunder. I now pronounce you husband and wife," Reverend Salley announced. "You may kiss the bride."

Serge pulled back Teresa's veil, cupped her chin in

his hand and kissed her as she stood on tiptoe. Warmth spread through his body like the dancing flame of the candle.

As the strings of the violin quivered, he joined hands with Teresa, and they led waiting friends and family out of the church to the awaiting cars. A procession of vehicles converged on Chez Gervais where they were greeted by proper waiters and shown to tables covered in spotless, white linen. Hors d'oeuvres on trays were served to the guests: escargot, French cheeses, stuffed mushroom caps, asparagus wrapped in bacon. Small glasses of red and white wine were circulated, and toasts were offered to the bride and groom.

The one given by Monsieur la Salle brought tears to Teresa's eyes.

"To the bride and groom, whom I love as a son and daughter," he said in his deep nasal accent. "May they have many joyous years together, and may their love ever burn bright. May they be blessed with children so that I can act as *grandpère*!"

"And *grandmère*," Marie echoed.

"To Serge and Teresa." Guy lifted his glass, and everyone drank to the couple's happiness.

The meal that followed offered a choice of chateaubriand or duck *à l'orange* created by the head chef. Afterward, there was the cutting of the cake, a three-tiered replica of the Eiffel Tower. Serge couldn't wait to be alone with his new bride though he was having a great time with friends and well-wishers.

As the two violinists and accordion player began to play a waltz, he swept Teresa onto the dance floor, for their first dance as a married couple. The overt affection that the couple shared as they held each other's gaze, stunned the guests into silence, and for a moment, even Teresa forgot that there was anyone else in the room but the two of them. Her dress swept around her like a graceful, drifting cloud. In a sweeping turn, Serge even lifted her feet from the ground. They looked as though they been created just for one another, to dance and move together in perfect synchronicity.

Behind them through the panoramic window, glowed the lights of Paris and the top of the Eiffel Tower. And higher in the midnight blue sky, the stars crisscrossed like a celestial bridge spanning the past and joining it to the future. A crescent moon reflected on the Seine shining on the City of Lights, on ancient cathedrals and modern architecture.

Polite applause erupted when they finished, and then other couples joined them: Guy and Annette, Monsieur la Salle and his rotund wife, Mauricette and the gangly young man she had invited as her date.

Serge whispered into her ear, and the warmth of his breath made her tingle with delight.

"Now you will always be my little bird," he said.

"Always," she replied, kissing him with ardent abandon.

"*Toujours.*"

## A word about the author...

Katherine McDermott has worked as an English teacher, guidance counselor, and adjunct English professor. She loves reading. She is married with two children and two adorable grandchildren.

In her spare time, like Teresa in *HIDING,* she likes to paint with acrylics. She received the Excellence in Christian Writing Award from the Blue Ridge Christian Writers Conference, the Daphne du Maurier award for an unpublished suspense novel, and honorable mention in the SOLA Romance Writers Conference.

She has written both fiction and non-fiction for magazines and newspapers. She is the author of two children's books, *The Underwear Tree* and *Les Petits Gardes*. She co-authored *The Lighthouses of S.C.*, wrote *All Work, All Play*, and has authored two plays.